Running

Scarred

By
Jackie Williams

Front Cover Photography

Natalie Williams
Cloverleaf Designs

This book is dedicated to all the men and women whose sacrifice keeps us safe every day

CONTENTS

With my everlasting love and thanks to my   wonderful daughter Natalie without whose patience and dedication, none of my books would have been possible.

Chapter One

The dead leaves rustled wildly under her stamping feet. This was the third time the woman had marched along the same path. Her pace hadn't lessened a beat from the first time she had pounded past his astonished eyes. He waited silently, hidden by a thick veil of ivy, wondering how long she was going to keep the punishing pace up.

He had been disturbed from his dinner by all the noise she was making. He had been about to enjoy the first mouthful of his homemade beef and mushroom pie and a glass of fine local red wine, when he had first heard the din.

It was an inexplicable sound. Crashing and rampaging violently through the usual evening calm.

Normally the forest that surrounded his cottage was quiet. He liked the serenity of the dark trees. Within the first two weeks of living there, he had learned to pick out the sounds of animals foraging and owls hunting. Now he could tell the difference between a deer brushing gently through the shrubbery and the wind whistling through the treetops.

He had been there for nearly two years, and he was absolutely certain that he had never heard this sort of noise before. This racket had worried him but he had calmly laid his knife and fork down, put his dinner in the oven to keep warm, opened his front door and had gone out into the gathering dusk to investigate.

Before he had seen her, he had assumed there was, at the very least, a herd of escaped cattle charging through the overgrown estate. He could scarcely believe his eyes when he had seen just one lone woman. She was so young and slender, he would have thought it impossible for someone as petite to make this raging cacophony of sound. She would normally be pretty too, he suspected, but she was obviously extremely angry and at this moment, she just looked hot, sweaty and annoyed.

Her legs were pumping hard, arms thrashing wildly at her sides. She was puffing clouds of breathy condensation into the cool evening air. It wafted about her shoulders, trying to keep up with her frantic pace, and then disappeared, swirling away into the darkening gloom of the forest.

Her long hair was being caught by the bushes and mud was spattering up the legs of her jeans. She was muttering angrily, her brow creased in annoyance, and he wondered how many more times she would go round in a circle before she realized her mistake. He kept to the shadows and watched as she stomped into the distance yet again.

He sighed deeply, knowing that he would probably end up having to lend a hand. He couldn't possibly let her walk round and round all night. He waited until he heard her storming off into the distance and then quietly moved a log across the path behind her. He pulled a huge mound of ivy from a nearby tree and banked it up behind the log. The next time she went round she would have to take a different route.

Damn Justin! This was the final insult. He had gone too far!

Ellen's breath was coming in great gasps of fury, huge fluffy clouds puffing out of her nose and mouth like an over worked steam train. The forest was full of the sound of her anger, the leaves rustling and twigs crackling under her boots, brambles snatching at her thick dark hair, ripping away from the earth and clinging with sharp thorns, trying to hold her back.

Exactly as if Justin was holding her back. She wasn't having it. Not anymore. She wrenched her hair away from the clawing stems and tried to walk more slowly, willing herself to calm down. The chilled, damp air was creeping through her overheated body and she still had a way to go. If she didn't slow down and control herself, she would be sweating and then in a short while she would be freezing.

She stopped for a few seconds, to gather her

breath and she listened to the quiet calm that surrounded her. Everything was suddenly so still and silent, far more silent than it had seemed a few moments before. It took almost a whole minute for her to realize that she had been the one making all the noise. She shivered in the stillness, listening to the hushed sounds of the forest. For a moment, she imagined it was breathing with her, its heart beating in the same rhythm as her own. She could almost feel the inner sounds of the trees, their living pulse beating in their thick branches. They sighed and yawned as they swayed in the evening breeze and she breathed with them, calming herself as she picked a few stray leaves from her now tangled hair.

She took a deep breath and marched on, pulling the overgrowth out of her way and following the faint muddy path beneath her feet.

Five kilometers, the sign had said. She reckoned she had marched a good three, and at a furious pace too. Her calves were aching and she had a painful stitch burning beneath her ribs. She pressed her hand to her side and puffed out miserably, gritting her teeth audibly. It was time to dig in and trudge the next two.

She looked upwards through the forest canopy. The bare branches above her hardly moved, though the air sung through the tops of the trees. She could see heavy clouds racing across the evening sky and she hoped it wouldn't start to rain. It wasn't quite dark on the path as most of the trees were still without their spring leaves, but there wasn't much daylight left. She estimated another half an hour of hard going and she checked her watch to confirm the time. It was getting difficult to see the hands. She didn't want to be out here at night time. Not that she was far from civilization and not that she was scared of the dark. Things like that didn't bother Ellen. She loved secret dark places. Always mysterious, always inviting.

But tonight she had a reservation at the hotel restaurant. Warm and cosy, dimly lit, with enticing smells and flavours. A gastronomic delight. She was always fascinated when a seemingly random selection of ingredients almost thrown together resulted in something delicious, tantalizing, something she wanted to linger on her tongue, savoured for far longer than chewing time allowed.

Her mother had never been much of a cook and Ellen hadn't had the time, money or the patience to learn after her parents had gone. Her strapping brother David, a Captain in the Royal Engineers, had only needed quantity and she was no shrinking violet when it came to food either. She had only ever dished up piles of sausages and steaming mash or vast amounts of roast dinners.

Her stomach rolled loudly at the thought of

the hotel chef's next spectacular creation. She didn't want to be late, even though it would mean sitting across the table from Justin. He may have been fabulously handsome, but his conversation no longer interested her. He was too wrapped up in himself, in his own plans to listen to anything she might say. She fumed all over again as she knew she was heading for a tasty but interminably dull evening.

When she thought about it seriously, she didn't even know why she was with him any longer. What little passion there had been, had fizzled out long ago, and since she had come into money, things had become even worse. It was as though he had become a habit, a very bad one that she had only continued because she was lonely with no one else at home.

She had only just finished a degree course in business, when news of the vast legacy had come through. She had done her utmost to remain unaltered by her new wealth, still keeping up her interests, seeing all her friends and cooking vast dinners for all of her brother's army pals, but it was difficult to contain the excitement. She had just bought a fabulous new car, one that Justin adored and they had been about to open their own designer boutique in her hometown when her life changed forever.

David had been blown up by a roadside

bomb while on duty in Afghanistan. His injuries were terrible. He had barely escaped with his life.

The money paled into insignificance instantly. She stopped the opening of the boutique and sold the ridiculous car. She left the money in the bank and set about helping her brother cope with his new and more restricted lifestyle.

David hadn't taken easily to being inactive. He was bitter, unresponsive, sometimes even aggressive, for many months afterwards, but then, as his rehabilitation had ended, the army had offered him a job in intelligence. He had leapt at the chance and had gone merrily back to an office job within his regiment, leaving Ellen unsure of what to do next.

And Justin had sulked ever since. He had loved the few weeks of luxury that her inheritance had brought him. He wanted the cars, the clothes, the holidays. He was no longer content to be seen rummaging through vintage clothes shops or to listen to rock music on their iPods, as they took long walks in the country. He dragged her into outrageously expensive restaurants or planned visits to the Venice Opera House. He sneered at her efforts on his dinner plate and avoided David and his colleagues like the plague.

That was what hurt her the most.

Justin could barely even look at David on his visits home, and he wouldn't be seen dead with him in public.

Her vast bank deposits took on another meaning for her now. She was not going to let it be frittered away on meaningless baubles that only bolstered one's own ego, but in something special and lasting, something that would benefit many. She put in hours of research and had come up with a fabulous idea. It had the enormous advantage of not having to make a profit. She didn't need any more money, she only needed the plan to not make a loss.

Justin had been furious when she had spoken to him of her French dream. She had explained her plan carefully. He knew the reasons behind it, but he had just gawped at her as though she were mad. He told her in hard angry tones, while they were eating a dish of overpriced, tasteless vongolè, that she knew nothing about property development and that she would never make a penny.

Not that he knew anything about property either, but at least Ellen had done the research.

He couldn't comprehend why she wanted to do it. He didn't understand that she wanted something that would be a completely new adventure.

Justin's idea of an adventure was somewhere between Marbella and Malaga, laying flat on his back on some over hot beach, having his drinks handed to him by scantily clad waitresses. And it turned out that his business acumen was even more mundane.

He had interpreted her ideas in his own shallow way and come up with seaside apartments and golfing duplexes in Spain. He had been thrilled when she had stopped trying to make him expand his horizons and given in to his brow beating. She remembered how her heart had thudded dully as she signed the million pound contract, knowing that the overpriced two bedroom duplexes overlooking an over manicured eighteenth fairway, would be a huge mistake. She hated having to be there to oversee them and Justin certainly wasn't interested in the work involved or in the people they had to employ to service them. It was becoming a nightmare.

And now he was trying the same thing in France. Justin was convinced he knew exactly what she wanted and he had dragged her around a selection of the most unsuitable apartments.

This time she wasn't going to give in. When she had been a teenager, her own mother had moaned endlessly about how stubborn she could be. Almost driven, when she had the bit between her teeth. Well, now Justin was going to get some of the same treatment.

For goodness sake, she was twenty-five. It was about time she took control!

She had been sitting on her fortune for over three years. She would spend it exactly as she liked.

If he didn't like her decision, and really thought the place they had just seen was such a great idea, then it was about time he put his own money where his mouth was.

She set her jaw determinedly and walked on briskly.

The path at her feet widened slightly and turned where an old ivy covered log had fallen. She didn't have to shove brambles out of her way as often now, but the air was becoming even cooler and the dusk was beginning to settle. She quickened her pace again, driving onwards, the pain in her shins now stabbing sharply.

She burst through the dense greenery and realized that she was pushing through a huge hedge of rhododendrons. Their thick, leathery leaves slapped her face as she scrambled through the bush.

Surely, she must have missed her way.

The path had been clearly marked not five minutes ago, and now it was completely overgrown. She felt as though she had been walking for hours.

She stumbled over hidden roots, tangled over the rough ground and at last staggered out into some sort of a clearing. She stood with her heart hammering as she surveyed the wide open area, wonder where her next marker would be and if she would ever be able to find it in the thickening gloom.

It took a moment for her eyes to adjust and take in the fantastic sight before her.

Weathered stone seemed to spring up everywhere in front of her. It towered over her and around her, great high walls barring her way, never-ending as they loomed into the distance. She ran towards the soaring mound of grey and pressed her hands against the flat surface, trying to ascertain if it were real or imaginary. It felt as solid and as cool as stone could possibly be and she placed her cheek against the cold smoothness, catching her breath as she tried to peer along its length into the increasing darkness.

A greying veil of algae covered the mighty Chateau walls. She stretched her arms along the arcing curve of a huge corner tower and she had to cling on hard to the cold stone to stop the sensation of upside down vertigo as she stared up at the overwhelming sight.

She took a massive, calming breath. She stepped backwards again to take in the spectacle, nearly falling into the rhododendrons she had just escaped from, and surveyed the length of the wall before her. It was a fairytale castle of vast proportions, the towers scrapping the sky on each corner. She was lost in its beauty as she stood gasping in delight. And then the dark grey clouds parted and a soft moonlight skimmed the walls and turrets.

It was a sorry sight. Certainly no fairytale. More like gothic horror. The roof had obviously collapsed in places and slipped tiles littered the ground. The massive walls gave way to drooping shuttered windows along its length, the frames soft with rot and spilling shattered glass that crunched under her feet as she walked along the surrounding path.

"Wow!" She breathed aloud, her awestruck whisper echoing off the stone. "What a fantastic find. It's nowhere on the maps." She was talking to herself as she dragged her fingers along the wall towards a wide set of stone steps that led her up to the high front door.

There was a small sign tacked to the wooden doors that filled the impressive stone arch.

"Entre Interdit. Danger!"

She pressed her forehead against the glass panel still hanging in the rotten wood at the side of the huge door, and tried to see through the filth. It was impossible. The light had faded so fast that it was becoming hard to see her hand in front of her face, let alone anything else. She stepped back and her foot slid on what she at first thought was a moss covered flagstone, but her foot kept sliding and she realized she was standing on a smooth sheet of damp cardboard. She staggered slightly, nearly slipping down the steps. She lifted her foot, but the cardboard had stuck to the mud on the sole of her boot and she ended up picking it off and throwing it back towards the floor, shaking sticky earth from her fingers. The cardboard caught on the hem of her jeans and tumbled down the steps, coming to land on the grass below.

She watched it fall and was about to turn away when she noticed the big white lettering, still clearly visible in the gloom, on the cardboard

"A Vendre"

My God! She thought wildly, as her imagination kicked in. *This place is for sale!*

She jumped back down the steps and grabbed the piece of sodden card. Her own muddy footprints obscured the name of the agent, making it too difficult to read in the ever-decreasing light. She wiped the card on the scrubby grass at her feet. "Agence Le Cam" There was a number beneath the name, small and ingrained with dirt. She folded the card across the middle and shoved it inside the neck of her jacket. She would decipher it later and then come back when she could see properly. She stood back to gaze up at the ruined Chateau once again and then turned back towards the forest, ready to face the rest of her walk.

The thick shrubbery gazed back at her

impenetrably. She had no idea of where she had come from and it was now so dark she could barely see at all.

She stood contemplating the leafy shrubs for a few moments and then walked along the edge of the line of rhododendrons, trying to spot a footpath marker or even where she had blundered through previously. There was nothing on this side of the Chateau and she squinted into the darkness as she came to the corner arcing tower of the vast building again. She turned and looked back towards the front door, momentarily confused.

Had she come from this side at all? It was all so symmetrical she really had no idea of which way to turn. She went back to the steps of the front door and stood very still, trying to get her bearings.

The dusk was fast becoming full dark and the near silence of the woods surrounded her, whispering tired sounds as the day came to an end. The only other sound came from her own jagged breathing and the loud thumping of her heart. She knew it was irrational. Even if she did have to stay here until the morning, it wouldn't be so bad. It really only meant a chilly, damp night camping and she had had plenty of those in her youth, when she had been a girl guide.

She would miss her fabulous dinner and Justin might be worried, but as she had stormed off, leaving him standing open mouthed beside the stunned estate agent, she could hardly expect him to have mounted a search party. He was probably sitting, relaxed at the hotel bar, starting on the first of his vodka and tonics. She put her hand in her pocket to find her phone, but then stopped as she clearly remembered leaving her mobile in the car because there was no signal

"Damn, what a fool!" She muttered to herself crossly, but she secretly knew that she probably wouldn't have telephoned Justin for help. She wouldn't want to give him the satisfaction.

She rubbed the patch of filthy glass again and pressed her face close, wondering if she wouldn't be better off inside the Chateau, but she could only make out a tiny patch of damp floor before it gave way to impenetrable inky black. She could see shards of shattered windows winking in the moonlight and then nothing. She suddenly felt that she would rather stay outside than attempt to get in. At least she wouldn't be in danger of cutting herself out here.

She squatted and then eased herself down onto the top step, staring away from the doors, into the darkness. The hard flagstones were cold under her backside and it wasn't long before she was shivering almost uncontrollably. She thought again about trying to find her way through the trees, but she had no idea of where to start, and short of stumbling through the forest all night long, without any guarantee of finding civilization, she was better off staying put, cold or otherwise.

She tried to make herself more comfortable, pressing her back into the corner of the stone doorway where it met the outside wall and rubbing the tops of her arms briskly, she attempted to regain some of the heat of her march. She closed her eyes, tucked her chin into her chest and wished the hours away, not thinking of the luxurious mattress and fluffy quilt waiting at her hotel.

But the thought of the warm covers was too much and, in a sort of waking dream, she pulled the fluffy down duvet over her now freezing shoulders and huddled into the Chateau entrance.

It was only as she heard the heavy breathing, breathing very unlike Justin's that she realized that somebody was right beside her and that a thick coat had been thrown across her body.

She sat bolt upright and tried to catch her breath as she saw the shape of a well-built man looming over her. He staggered backwards, surprised at her sudden movement and the darkness disguised his features for a moment. Then the moon appeared from behind a cloud and she caught a glimpse of an almost familiar, handsome but ragged face, pale in the moonlight, shadowed or perhaps wrinkled strangely on one side, with glinting sapphire eyes peering at her from under long dark hair. Another cloud raced across the moon again and everything was plunged into darkness.

She scrabbled back into the corner as far as she was able, but he leaned in towards her, tall and heavy across the shoulders. She felt his breath, warm and garlicky, waft over her. He reached out his hand as she opened her mouth to ask who he was, and put a warm palm gently across her trembling lips. He muttered in a hoarse whisper.

"Shhh. I'm not going to hurt you. Come with me. I'll take you to the road."

He waited for just a moment, checking that she had understood him, before he took his hand away from her mouth again and grappled at the top of her arm. She swallowed dryly as he pulled her gently upright. She caught another hint of garlic and something that smelled like fresh herbs. Rosemary maybe? It wasn't unpleasant. It was delicious. She was so caught up in his scent that she didn't realize for a moment that he had spoken to her in English.

He towered over her, the dark shadows of the Chateau masking his true outline, his forceful presence electrifying the air all around her. And then she noticed he was favouring one side as he dragged her, with a slightly uneven lope, down the stone steps. She twisted away from his grasp as they reached the rough grass and she stared towards him, willing the clouds out of the way.

She wanted to see him clearly. She wanted to know who this Englishman was. The clouds moved across the sky in a thick blanket of darkest grey. Ellen was about to turn across the front of the Chateau, but he caught hold of her again, his huge hand encircling her upper arm firmly, fiery heat penetrating through her flimsy jacket. He began pushing her towards the even darker leaves of the forest. It was several seconds before she found her voice.

"Stop! I'm fine, you don't need to hold me. I don't need your help." She could hear the slight tremor in her own voice, though she wasn't afraid.

The man gave a gravelled grunt, and then what may possibly have been a laugh. He let go of her arm suddenly and caught the edge of the coat still draped around her shoulders then, in another hoarse whisper, he growled.

"If you want to stay out in the cold all night then fine, I'll leave you here, but I guess you'd rather go back to your hotel." His voice was deep, rasping in the back of his throat, his words punctuated with breathy swallows, but she noticed the accent. Very much like her own, often mistaken by the French for London, but really Essex.

She was so taken aback that she stopped

struggling and let him pull her through the undergrowth. It took her a few more minutes of being dragged along through the now pitch black forest, before she had the breath to speak again

"I need to get to Plestin. I know it's not far but I have to admit that I'm slightly disorientated. Do you know the way?" She kept her eyes on the space above her. Although she could see virtually nothing, she looked at where she could hear the sound of his breathing, steady and firm.

There was a low throaty laugh at her ear and the man let go of her entirely. For a second she was lost in the inky dark, she whimpered as she stretched out her hands, blindly batting air until he caught her arm again. He laughed once again. His tone was more normal now. Not nearly so gruff. It was as though he was getting used to using his own voice.

"I know the way better than you, and you obviously do need my help. I said I'd take you as far as the road. We're nearly there. Can you see the lights yet? You've got about another half mile after you reach them, but if I point you the right way you should be able to manage that on your own even with your terrible sense of direction." As insulted as she was she kept quiet. Something in his tone made her thrill and shiver and want to hear him again. His voice was warm and as deep as his breathing, but he was silent now as he guided her further onwards.

She caught the hint of a perfume, rich and spicy. She breathed it in deeply and closed her eyes. And then a sudden feeling of complete arousal nearly overcame her. A feeling that she hadn't had for years and with an intensity she had never experienced before. She clamped her lips together as incredibly erotic sensations shot through her body. She balled her hands into tight fists, almost afraid that she would say something or even do something regrettable. She felt almost faint as his muscled arm brushed past her cheek as he pointed in front of her.

He spoke again, this time his voice melted over her, thick and velvety.

"There, see them now? The lights along the road."

She couldn't answer and she didn't look at his hand, she didn't want to see the lights. She could feel her heart pounding against her ribs and she knew that she wanted to stay with him here in the dark forest.

What the hell was the matter with her? He was a complete stranger. A hobo, obviously living rough in these woods, maybe a tramp who sheltered in the Chateau. Not some Prince Charming about to sweep her off her feet. And why would she want a Prince Charming anyway? She had Justin. Her heart plummeted and she shook herself back to reality, pushing this strange man's husky, secret tones into the back of her mind as she stared ahead, straining her eyes into the endless darkness and seeing nothing at all. He guided her further along the path, his body so close to hers that she could feel the heat pulsing from him.

Another twenty paces she could see pinpoints of light in the distance. Relief surged through her. She wasn't sure if it was relief to see the lights or relief that she could now move away from his intoxicating presence. She breathed out a huge lungful of air.

"Yes, I can see them now. I knew I was near the town. I was just disorientated. Thank you so much." She turned towards the man at her elbow, but his warmth was no longer at her side and she realized that he was already gone. She stood still for a few seconds, feeling horribly empty and cold, listening to the small, whispering sounds of the forest moving gently as someone pushed their way through the undergrowth, and then there was complete silence again. "Thanks Essex boy!" She yelled playfully out into the dark.

From further away than she would have imagined possible in the few short moments he had left her, she heard a faint.

"No problem, Essex girl. Night." There was a slight laugh in his deep tones.

She peered after the beautiful voice for a

long moment, strangely glad that he had known her accent too, and then she turned back toward the lights of the town and walked briskly along the main road.

She skipped up to the wide entrance of her hotel, about to push through the heavy glass doors when she realized she was still holding the overcoat the man had thrown over her. She clasped it tightly around her shoulders. It was made of a heavy khaki material with a furred lining, thick and warm and she breathed in the fabulous, woodsy smell of it. She stood for a second on the threshold of the hotel and turned back towards the forest wondering where he lived.

Would he be missing it? She didn't know whether to run back and call out to him again. But then she heard raised voices coming from inside the hotel foyer, and recognizing one of them, she turned to the glass doors to see a glowering Justin, red in the face, shouting furiously at the hapless receptionist.

The man was watching the hotel entrance, invisible amongst the thick shrubbery. He stood quietly, his eyes fixed upon her from the opposite side of the road. He saw her march up to the wide glass doors, shoulders tight, back straight and then she stopped and looked back to the road for a second. She seemed to shrink in on herself for a moment but then she shook her shoulders, pushed the door open with a determined shove and disappeared inside.

He drew his eyebrows together, a little confused. She hadn't sounded at all unhappy as he had marched her through the forest but she had been frowning as she had approached the hotel and, if he wasn't mistaken, she didn't look as though she really wanted to be there.

He had turned away from her as she had seen the lights along the road and had melted back into the bushes to go home. He had only doubled back and kept watch over her to make sure she wasn't stupid enough to turn the wrong way when she reached the junction. And then, quite suddenly, as her perfume stole about him again, warm and succulent in the night chill, he had not wanted to let her out of his sight. He forgot about his dinner congealing in his oven and walked parallel to her, keeping in step, as he remained hidden by the thick screen of bushes. He caught another hint of her scent as he watched her slender figure striding out purposefully.

He had been impressed when she sat down by the door of the Chateau. He had hoped she would be able to find her way to the hotel after he had altered the route of the path. It was quite direct if you knew where to start.

It was obvious that she didn't have a clue.

She had missed it completely, not noticing the marker as she ploughed through the undergrowth around the Chateau.

He had thought that she was going to dissolve into a sudden deluge of tears, but to his complete surprise, she had just sighed, in a resigned sort of way, brushed a few leaves away from around where she was going to sit and had squatted down. She was asleep almost immediately.

He had nearly laughed out loud at her gentle snoring, her hair falling all about her shoulders and lifting slightly as she breathed rhythmically. She had looked almost comfortable, tucked against the cold stone. Certainly not scared. He had been about to leave her there, when she had given an involuntary shiver as she nodded gently. It rolled right through her body and he knew he couldn't leave her, cold and unattended for the entire night.

If she hadn't woken as he'd placed his coat over her, he would have just kept an eye on her, but he thought that she had been about to scream at him and he didn't want her to do that. He hated screaming. He had heard enough screaming to last him a lifetime and he didn't think her being a woman, would make it any easier for him to bear. He placed his hand as gently as he could over her mouth.

Her breath had whispered through his fingers, warm and moist and her eyes had opened wide. He took hold of her arm, steadying her as she wobbled down the stone steps.

Her arm had felt thin, not skinny, but strong and tightly muscled under his hand. She had wrenched herself away from him with unexpected strength. He'd stared at her curiously in the darkness, seeing her tumbling hair, dark against the smooth, pale skin of her face. She glimmered softly in the moonlight. Her huge dark eyes sparkled under heavy black lashes as she stared up at him. In the fading light he couldn't decide if they were brown or green. Whichever was the case, it didn't matter. He knew he had made a huge mistake.

He had stood stunned.

She was utterly beautiful.

He breathed deeply as he thought of her wide eyes, and a strange constricting sensation gripped his chest.

She hadn't recoiled from him and he had assumed that she hadn't or couldn't see his terrible face. Maybe she needed glasses, or maybe she just couldn't see well in the dark, she hadn't seen the streetlights for minutes after they were visible to him. He felt relieved, his vile features were not something that anybody would want to see unexpectedly.

He rubbed his hand over the side of his face and recoiled from himself. The disgusting waxy feeling, cold and hard and unnatural was still there, a constant reminder of how careless he had been. He flexed his square jaw for a brief moment, then dropped his hand to his side and sighed miserably. It was nothing he could fix and at least she hadn't appeared to notice. He was glad that she hadn't seen him clearly. He hated the way people reacted to the way he looked. Either a grim determination not to look away from him, smile fixed on their horrified lips, or an embarrassed glance down, then a flick back to his eyes before they looked anywhere else but his face. For the last two years he had stayed hidden away in the forest, avoiding contact with others as much as possible.

He watched her carefully through the hotel doors for a few moments longer, feeling slightly uneasy as he saw her talking to a good-looking blond man. He smiled grimly when she didn't look very pleased to see the man. She turned away from the looker sharply and stalked up the wide staircase beside the foyer.

He sighed as she disappeared from his view. The man at the desk was obviously her lover, however displeased she appeared to be by seeing him. He had noted her lack of wedding band almost immediately.   Not that her wearing of a wedding band or not would ever concern him. He turned and sighed deeply as he trudged, back towards his house in the woods, pushing the undergrowth out of his way as he stomped unevenly along the familiar but nearly invisible path.

It was only when a thick stemmed bramble tore painfully at his shoulder, scragging his skin through his shirt, that he realized that the woman still had his coat. He stopped and turned back for a second, wondering if he dared go and ask for it, but then he shrugged, it wasn't that cold. He'd seen her pick up the "For Sale" sign at the Chateau and had heard her breathe out "Fantastic." She would obviously be back and with a bit of luck, she would bring his coat. He wasn't entirely adverse to the idea, she was certainly lovely to look at, and he wanted to look at her again.

He wouldn't mind hearing her soft voice again either. Funny how they had both recognized the Essex accent. The few people in France that he'd had the courage to talk to seemed to think he came from the East End of London. She had a graceful, educated tone and he wondered where she came from exactly. Not Dagenham, that was for sure. He took a deep breath. It wasn't as if he was going to ask her. If she did bother to bring back his coat, he would have to be careful and stay out of sight. He hadn't scared her tonight but it wouldn't be so easy to remain invisible during the daytime.

He gave an unexpected shudder as he imagined the look on her face if she ever saw his, and he hoped fervently that it would never happen.

Chapter Two

"Do you have any idea of who I am? I want the police called now! It's dark and she could have wandered anywhere. She has no sense of direction at all. The cliff is only a few hundred meters away. You'll take the blame if any harm comes to her." Justin's voice was carrying all around the hotel. Several other guests had stopped in the reception area to stare at him.

The receptionist sighed in relief as she saw Ellen walking towards them. She smiled broadly and spoke in heavily accented English.

"Actually Monsieur, I 'ave no idea of who you are but it is of no consequence anyway, she is 'ere now. She 'as not been lost. You 'ave made an error. I think she 'as just been for a walk." She added as she looked down at the mud on Ellen's jeans.

Justin was about to bluster in fury again but then he looked over his shoulder at Ellen as she trudged towards him. Ellen smiled graciously at the receptionist and then raised her eyebrows at her fiancé. His handsome face was blotched red, his normally perfect hair dishevelled.

Ellen snorted in indignation.

"Well thanks for that vote of confidence Justin! No sense of direction indeed! I'm going to shower. I'll see you for drinks in half an hour, if you think I'll be able to find my way back down the stairs by myself." She whispered sarcastically as she turned sharply towards the wide staircase and without looking back, stalked up to their suite, ignoring his shocked expression and the trail of mud and leaves that she left in her wake. Justin shook his head and followed her up to their room a few minutes later. He shoved the key card into the lock and barged into their suite. Ellen was tugging off her clothes and piling them on the bed.

"For God's sake Ellen! What the hell is wrong with you? First you act grumpy for half the day, then you shout at me and stalk off in front of the agent. I felt a right idiot. What is it with you this week? Is it your period or something?" He was standing at the end of the bed, glaring at her as she pulled off the last of her muddy clothes.

She stood in her bra and pants and stared at him open mouthed for a moment.

"That's low Justin, even for you. And believe me I wasn't acting grumpy. I was grumpy, furious in fact, and do you blame me?" She grabbed a towelling dressing gown from the back of a chair and wrapped it tightly around her. "I had explained exactly what I was looking for and you told me that you had arranged several viewings. I didn't realize that you had completely ignored my wishes yet again. Am I meant to be happy when you do that?

I'd rather be told that there was nothing suitable to view." She glared right back at him.

Justin fiddled with the heavy gold cufflinks at his slim wrists.

"Well, I didn't think you were serious. It's such a stupid idea. It'll cost a bomb to set up and you'll never see a penny return. I just don't see the point. I know you have your reasons, but they are irrational. Even your brother David said you must be mad. If you listened to me…" He tailed off at her livid expression.

She turned towards the bathroom and spoke over her shoulder furiously.

"When was the last time you spoke to David? You can barely look at him when he comes home, let alone have any kind of conversation. He thinks what I'm doing is a fabulous idea and I'm going to go ahead with it whether you like it or not. I would have thought you knew by now that this project doesn't have to make money. It only has to cover basic costs to keep it going, and David is in full agreement. It's my money Justin and I'll do whatever I want with it…I'm showering and then going to bed. If you want dinner then you'll have to eat on your own. You've put me off my food completely. In fact, why don't you go and book another room. I really don't want to sleep with you tonight."

Justin shoved her dirty clothes across the covers and sat down heavily on the end of the bed. He flicked the arm of her dressing gown as she swept past.

"You don't have to be so dramatic Ellen. Look, we've had a busy couple of days and we're both tired. Shower and then come and eat with me." His voice softened and he stood up again, as she stopped. He put a hand tentatively on her shoulder and took it as a good sign that she didn't shake him off. "Where were you Ellen? You know how I worry. I was really scared. I thought something bad had happened to you." He was whispering into her ear.

She turned to face him, moving out of his reach, not able to deal with the strange emotions that were still racing through her body at this precise moment. She didn't want him snuggling up to her. She didn't want him at all. But she kept those feelings to herself. Perhaps this wasn't the best time to bring up her thoughts about parting.

"Oh Justin! You idiot. I can walk along a footpath by myself. You don't have to worry about me all the time." She crossed her fingers in the pockets of the dressing gown and put the feelings of panic at being lost to the back of her mind. She certainly wasn't going to tell him that she had resigned herself to a night of camping and was only back at the hotel now because of the help of a tall, dark stranger. She shivered slightly at the thought of the man's hand on her arm, but it wasn't a cold shiver. It was a shiver of unexplained pleasure. She nearly groaned out loud as her heart began to beat in an uneven rhythm.

Justin stepped forwards and giving her no choice, he pulled her into his chest, murmuring into her hair.

"Of course I have to worry about you. That's what fiancé's do." He pulled a leaf from her tangled hair. "And it's obvious that you needed worrying over. I can't believe I let you stomp off like that. Anything could have happened to you. People get to hear things. If they know there's a multi-millionairess on the loose, you could be in big trouble. I should never have let you out of my sight." He felt her stiffen again in his arms and knew at once that he'd said the wrong thing.

She pulled away from him, angry all over again.

"You're the only one round here that knows about my wealth, unless you've gone and told anyone." She knew immediately, by the look on his face, that he had. She could just imagine him showing off in the bar. "And anyway, you don't own me Justin. I can do exactly as I wish. You can't stop me."

He pressed his lips together into a thin, hard line, then spoke again.

"Yes, I think you've made that quite plain Ellen. But as soon as we're married, I shall have to put my foot down. I can't have you embarrassing me like that again. The estate agent thought I was a complete idiot!" His tone was harsher now and he caught hold of her wrist as she stepped back to look up into his pale blue eyes.

He was smiling down at her as though he'd been joking, but the smile didn't quite reach the corners of his eyes and his grasp on her wrist was just a little too tight. She wrenched her hand away from him, but didn't move back any further. She lifted her chin slightly, her defiance obvious.

"Just let me take a shower Justin. Then perhaps I will feel like dinner after all. I don't want to argue about this now."

He bit his lip and clenched his hand at his side, fighting the urge to slap her haughty face.

"Who's arguing? I'm famished and you look as though you need a drink. Come on, hurry up and get showered and then we can eat." He sat down on the bed again as she walked into the bathroom and closed the door quietly.

She let the hot water run over her body for a long time, its heat warming her where her skin felt icy. It was an odd coldness, deeper than on the surface, chilling her to the bone. She hadn't felt cold inside the stranger's thick coat. Far from it. She had been as warm as toast. It was only as she had entered the hotel after seeing Justin's livid face that an icy blast had swept over her.

She looked down at her wrist where he had held her. There was a faint red mark on her skin. Nothing really, only a slight abrasion, but she could still feel the grip of his cold fingers. Had he meant to grasp her that hard?

She let her fingers wander higher up her arm to where the man in the woods had held her so gently as he had guided her. She tingled with a fiery heat and felt her heart begin to pound again as a strange quiver ran through her entire body. She took some deep breaths, trying to dismiss the ludicrous sensations. It couldn't be possible to feel this sensitized or aroused after meeting someone she could barely see, for less than half an hour.

She shampooed her hair twice and then conditioned it, letting the thick liquid linger while she soaped the rest of her body. The muscles in her calves were still tense from all the walking she had put herself through, and she massaged them firmly, hoping they wouldn't be as tight in the morning. She rinsed her hair again, turned off the water and stepped out of the cubicle to dry herself.

The steam wafted thickly about her and she knew it would be impossible to dry off in the damp atmosphere, but she still stood there, not wanting to leave the small room. She turned to brush her teeth over the sink and wiped the mirror with a clammy hand. She caught sight of the red marks on her wrist again as she dropped her hand and she stared at her reflection for a long second, before the glass misted over again. There was a faint line of concern above her eyebrows and as she saw it, she felt it deepen.

She looked down at her arm again and suddenly she definitely didn't want to leave the bathroom.

Justin had hurt her. She wasn't imagining it. He had done it deliberately!

Her gaze dropped to the door and she was suddenly relieved that she had locked it.

She sat on the edge of the bath wondering how she had let things go this far. She thought of the way he had organized the visits with the estate agent, dismissing her requests and submitting his own instead. She thought about the Spanish properties, how she had felt bullied into signing and how she had only noticed his name appearing on all the paperwork when it was all just a little too late. Although he hadn't paid a penny for the properties, his name was on all the deeds.

She had been afraid to ask why. But in her

heart she had already known. To all intents and purposes, he now owned half of all the golfing duplexes, maybe more. She was unsure of exactly how Spanish law related to unmarried couples, but she suspected that Justin would know exactly how much he would get if they were ever sold. *Was he trying to control her life and her money completely?*

She thought about the wedding dates he had suggested. All of them were in the horribly near future. She had felt more than relieved when each of his chosen venues had told them that they were booked until the following year. She felt uneasy that she was pleased he wanted a big wedding, a huge social occasion that took an extortionate amount of time and money to organize. She was more than relieved he didn't want to pop down to the local registry office to get married at a fortnights notice.

She looked at herself in the misty mirror again. The crease across her forehead looked set in stone now that she had thought of their prospective wedding.

She didn't want to marry him. It was a completely ridiculous idea. She couldn't believe that she had ever thought it possible. She would have to tell him soon that it was all off. She looked back at the crease on her forehead. If it wasn't going to become a permanent feature, she would have to tell him now.

She wrapped her hair in another towel and dragged the bathrobe about her shoulders, tying the belt as tight as possible. She took a deep steadying breath before she turned the handle of the door and stepped out to face him.

The bedroom was empty. Justin had obviously decided not to wait. She exhaled the great breath she had taken inside the bathroom and slumped onto the bed, shaking with relief. She had been more scared of confronting him than she had realized.

She rushed to the door and turned the lock before hanging the dressing gown on the hook on the door, then she walked back to the bed and sat down on the edge.

She pushed her clothes out of her way and was about to fall back onto the covers, when she noticed the strangers thick coat beneath her own jacket and jeans.

She pulled it out from under the pile of her dirty clothes. It was big and soft, the woodsy smell wafting around her as she lifted it to her face, breathing it in deeply. There was a herby, smoky taint to the fabric. She sniffed it in, liking the unusual scent as she wondered if the woodsman kept an open fire. The soft furry lining of the coat felt warm and comfortable and she scrunched her hands into the thick fabric, dragging it over her naked body and enveloping herself entirely in its huge depths. He hadn't asked for its return and she wondered how she could have forgotten to give it back to him. She snuggled into its warmth and hoped he wasn't missing it too much.

Suddenly she was rather glad that Justin hadn't spotted it under her pile of dirty clothes. She thought he had been too agitated to notice her wearing the unfamiliar garment when she had appeared at the reception desk. She picked it up and folded it over her arm then stood up and walked to the wardrobe. There were several plastic laundry bags on a shelf. She pulled one down, slipped the coat inside, and placed it on the floor of the wardrobe. She didn't want to hide the coat as that would only prove that she had something to hide, if it was discovered, but she hoped Justin wouldn't see it. She didn't want to have to explain it to him.

She would have to take the coat with her when she viewed the Chateau and hope that she saw the man again then. Her heart began to thump irrationally again. She gulped and made herself an excuse. She really only wanted to thank him for pointing her in the right direction, but then as she thought of Justin, cold and hard, waiting for her downstairs, she wished, in a very tiny compartment of her brain, that she had stayed out all night, sitting under the stars with the big, muscular man at her side. Safe and warm and protected.

She stood up at last and pulled clean underwear from a drawer, then she selected a dark purple dress from the rail and slipped it over her head, letting the fabric fall down her slender body. She turned to the dressing table and combed her still damp hair. She scraped it back from her face and plaited it quickly, fastening the end with a diamond clip that her brother David had given her for her last birthday.

It was a perfect copy of a paste hair clip he had given her on her eighteenth birthday. He had been twenty and heading off for his first tour of duty with his regiment. She was going to be on her own for the first time since their parents had died and she had wept as he'd given her the beautiful jewel. The original had been the most favourite present she had ever received and she wore it as often as possible. David had only suggested replacing it for her when he had noticed that a stone was missing and the metal was becoming tarnished. The only difference to the original was that the new copy was made of platinum and was set with clusters of flawless diamonds.

She brushed her lips with a fine layer of gloss and gave her already thick eyelashes a quick coat of mascara. She glanced into the mirror and decided she looked quite nice. Well, nice enough to tell someone that you no longer wanted to be with him. She hoped he wouldn't make too much of a scene. Especially not in public and certainly not before she had the chance to taste the chef's amazing cooking. She slipped on a pair of high heels and picked up her slim evening bag before opening up the room door and heading downstairs towards the bar.

Justin had waited in the bedroom for a little over five minutes. He was bored.

How long could it possibly take her to shower? Forever it seemed. His patience was running thin. Since she had inherited all her millions, she was a changed woman, getting all sorts of weird ideas about who should do what in their relationship.

And now this completely bonkers business plan, or project or whatever stupid name she wanted to call it. He could thank her repulsive brother David for that. If he hadn't come back from Afghanistan with his legs blown off and his face completely mangled, it would never have crossed her mind. They would now be running a fabulous designer boutique and driving round in fast cars. Justin wished heartily that David hadn't come back at all. He was almost as much of a nuisance as she was. Their pathetic joint venture was going to cost him a bomb in lost cash.

He stood up and walked impatiently to the dressing table, picking up one of Ellen's bits of horrible plastic jewellery. He glanced down at the hair clip in his hand. Her favourite piece, given to her by the hideous David when she was a teenager apparently. Not that he had been quite so hideous then.

Since he had last seen her wear it, she had obviously given the clip a bit of a clean-up and had shoved another stone in the gap where one had previously fallen out, but then she wore the damn thing so often, it was no wonder it was falling apart. Why, with all her millions, she couldn't replace it with something decent, he didn't know.

He regarded his handsome face in the mirror and smiled grimly at his reflection. Checking his hair and fingering his gold and diamond cufflinks. At least he looked a millionaire, even if he wasn't one…yet. He was on his way and only needed to have Ellen sign a few more properties over to him, and he would be set for life. Then he could get rid of the stupid cow and live happily ever after.

He gave a grim laugh. He couldn't really believe how stupid she was. She hadn't queried his name on the deeds of the Spanish apartments and he wanted to try the same thing again here in France. Property prices were incredibly cheap, there had to be room for a good profit.

He felt slightly odd when he thought of Ellen now. At one time, long before she had received her money, he had seriously believed that he loved her. But then it all became a bit dull. He hated rummaging around second-hand markets and going on filthy treks through mud soaked countryside with her. Their relationship had been coming to an end and he had been about to break it off with her, when she and David had announced that they been left a fortune by their great aunt.

Nobody had known the old bag had won a fortune on some European lottery. She hadn't spent a penny of it. The money was all just sitting there in a high interest account. Piles of it. And it had piled up even more over the ten years since she had won it. More money than he had ever dreamed of. All left to her great nephew and niece, just because they took a little time and trouble to visit her on the odd occasion and sometimes wrote her letters or sent postcards from their holidays. Her teenage grandson, who hadn't bothered contacting her for years, had been livid, but there was nothing he could do about it and Ellen and David had been very generous with their gifts to him even though the ungrateful little sod hadn't deserved a penny.

Justin had thought them both stupid then, each giving away half a million pounds to the little twit, and he hadn't revised his opinion. He hid it carefully, waiting patiently until he could get his hands on the rest of Ellen's share of the cash. He would be forever grateful that he hadn't ditched her before she had inherited the money. At least that was one thing he was very clear about. Even if he didn't love her, he certainly loved her money, and he wasn't going to pass up the chance of getting his hands on it.

He had even tried to arrange their wedding so that he would be assured of at least half of her inheritance after they married and then divorced, but sometimes even money couldn't talk. The best venues were booked years in advance and there was no way he was going to have an invisible wedding at some run of the mill registry office. If he was going to married to a millionairess, he wanted the whole world to know it. Just being her fiancé had reaped excellent rewards already and being married to her would bring even more. He could wait a little longer to have exactly the perfect venue.

Even he had to admit that Ellen wasn't pig ugly or anything, actually she was quite beautiful and she was pretty good in bed. Well, accommodating, she had never refused him at least. She had high, firm breasts and long slim legs that wrapped themselves satisfyingly about his waist as he made love to her. Made love! That was a laugh; thank God he didn't have to bother too often. She seemed quite happy with a quick session once or twice a month. He would have preferred her to be lustier and more dominant in bed, like the women he visited while in London, then he may have enjoyed himself a little more, but it was a small price to pay, and not a completely unpleasant one, to get his hands on her inheritance.

He looked towards the bathroom door and wondered if he should go in and have sex with her now, while she was in the shower. He hadn't liked the way she had spoken to him earlier. Maybe he should do it to her now, just to remind her who was the boss. It would save time later and make a pleasant change from her lying flat on her back. He ran his finger around the inside of his collar, thinking about her wet, slippery body, but then he just couldn't be bothered. He'd do it to her after dinner when they were getting undressed anyway.

He dropped the plastic clip carelessly back onto the dressing table. It made a surprisingly heavy clunk on the glass surface and he glanced up at the bathroom door in case she had heard. The shower was still running. He walked to the bedroom door and let himself out. He'd go and wait in the bar for her.

Maybe if she had a few glasses of wine, she'd be easier to handle and then perhaps he could try out some more interesting positions with her. He might as well enjoy it if he had got to do it.

Chapter Three

The sun was shining brightly through the bedroom windows. Justin pulled the quilt over his head to shut out the light, not for the first time hating the fact that the French never used curtains.

He could hear Ellen moving about the room, every tiny noise amplified by the pounding in his head. His mouth felt dry, his chest and stomach ached from the amount of times he'd vomited during the night.

"Can't you be quiet, Ellen. I've got a terrible hangover." He groaned weakly from under the covers.

All movements stopped in the bedroom and he pulled the quilt back to squint blearily into the sunshine. Ellen was standing by the bed, staring back at him. She was fully dressed, face made up and hair perfectly tousled, obviously ready to go out. A frown creased her forehead and her eyes glittered dangerously.

"Well if you hadn't drunk all that vodka and then all my wine, maybe you wouldn't be feeling so bad. Why don't you just stay there, I'm going out." She spoke sharply.

He struggled to sit up, suddenly furious at her tone of voice.

"Where in God's name are you off to so

early? We haven't any appointments for today Ellen."

She rolled her eyes in exasperation.

"It's not early Justin. I've already had breakfast. I brought you a couple of croissants just in case you could manage them." She indicated a plate on the bedside table.

The fury left him, to be replaced with revulsion as he saw the plate. The rich pastries were shiny with butter. She had put a big blob of raspberry jam at the side of them. It wobbled nervously as he pushed the plate further away. He swallowed and pulled the covers up again as his stomach churned. He didn't think he would be sick again. He had nothing left to be sick with, but he wasn't willing to risk it.

"Thanks, but no thanks." He mumbled feebly as he slumped back down in the bed.

Ellen stared, revolted, at him for another second and then picked up the bag at her feet. She took a quick glance at her reflection in the mirror and then turned back to Justin.

"I'm meeting that agent I told you about last night. He has something to show me that may be just what I'm looking for, but I'm going on my own. If the place is any good for my project, you wouldn't be interested and I don't want you there anyway. You can stay here and sleep your hangover off." Her voice still had the sharp edge to it and Justin struggled to look at her from under the edge of the duvet.

"For God's sake Ellen, can't you wait until I'm ready? Can't you wait until this afternoon at least? I could come with you and give some sort of level headed opinion. You're going to need it as you're so airy fairy and likely to get carried away otherwise." He barely knew why he was offering. He felt terrible. There was no way he was getting out of bed before lunchtime.

She stared at his outline under the covers and felt sick just looking at his curled, pathetic form. She couldn't believe she had stayed with him for so long or fathom how she had once thought him handsome. She must have been blind not to see all his faults before now. She wondered if this was the right time to bring up last night's conversation, unsure from how he was reacting, if he could recall what they had talked about.

"Justin, do you remember anything of what we discussed last night? Did you understand any of what I was telling you?"

He was silent for a moment and he brought his eyebrows together as he concentrated for a second, then he spoke hoarsely.

"To be honest I can't remember much of anything about last night, well, not after you came into the hotel looking as though you'd been dragged through a hedge backwards. Look, I might as well make it plain now. If you want to go ahead and look at this place, then fine, but there's no way you're going to get me involved in this ridiculous plan." He turned over in the bed then swallowed a couple of times as his stomach churned again at the sight of the pastries. Their sickly sweet aroma wafted across him and bile rose in his throat. He was in no fit state to have this argument.

Ellen looked at him in horror as she saw his skin turn a strange shade of green and she quickly swept the plate of croissants over to the dressing table.

"Justin! Don't you remember any of last night at all? I didn't even sleep in the same room as you. I booked another down the hall. You are not going to be involved in any of my plans any more. Not now or in the future." She sat down suddenly on the end of the bed, unexpected relief washing over her as the words rushed out. "It's over Justin. Until yesterday I thought there still might be a chance for us, but after what happened with the estate agent and last night. It brought everything to a head and made me realize how bad things are between us. I know that I've made the right choice. I'm sorry that you don't remember the conversation, but I made it plain. I don't want to be with you any longer."

He struggled to sit up, slightly confused still, but suddenly wide-awake. The thought of millions of pounds drifting from his grasp suddenly spurring him into action.

"You can't mean that! Just because of a difference of opinion over what sort of places we want to buy. Ellen, be reasonable for goodness sake. Surely we can come to some sort of agreement that will be good for both of us. I'll keep quiet about anything else until you've got your idea off the ground and then we can go look at some sensible property."

There it was again. Property. She knew she had made the right decision. She shrugged.

"But that's just it Justin. I am being reasonable. I let you influence me over Spain. I let you joint own the properties even though you put nothing in. Not even a moment of your time. It's me that's buying property for you because that's what you want, but those types of places hold no interest for me. And to be honest, I'm pretty sure you don't have any interest in me either. I think you are only interested in my money. You know how I feel about David and a lot of his friends, my friends. I grew up with them all, they all looked after me when our parents died. I needed them so much then, and now I'm in a position to do something about it, I can return the favour. It's obvious you have no concern for them at all."

He leaned forwards, ignoring his roiling stomach as he tried to take her hand, gripping it tightly, desperate to placate her.

"Ellen, how can you say that? Of course I feel for them, I'm not totally insensitive, but they signed up for this type of thing. They signed their lives away when they joined up so I don't see why I should feel that sorry for them. Let the government pay for it. It doesn't have to be you. You're going to spend all your money on this daft, sentimental project and get nothing back. It doesn't make any sense."

She sighed deeply. *Always the same. Money, money, money.* No feeling for her or for David and his friends. She pulled her hand out of his over tight, sweaty grasp.

"It may not make sense to you, but it does to me. Nobody signs up to have half their body ripped off Justin. None of them sign up to be disfigured by revolting, burning chemicals that some crazy war lord thinks are a necessity to keep his drug route open. I've put enough money away to live comfortably for the rest of my life and so I can spend the rest on other people if I want to." Her voice suddenly hardened. "And I think I've spent enough on you. While you were preoccupied in the loo last night, I came to a decision. I'm going to sign the

Spain thing over to you completely. A million pounds worth of property Justin. Think of it! All for you. I don't want anything to do with those apartments any longer, I never wanted them in the first place and...I definitely don't want anything more to do with you either. We're finished. I think the properties will be a good enough settlement for you, especially as, in law, I don't think I have to do anything at all for you." She stood up and moved towards the door.

He suddenly noticed her travelling case standing outside the wardrobe and, realizing at last that she was serious, began to pull the covers out of his way. His panic made his stomach roil even more.

"You decided all this just because I was drunk last night? You can't do this to me Ellen. We've been together for years. Don't I have a say in anything?" He stumbled, naked, out of the bed, but she opened the room door and stepped through into the corridor.

"You've had plenty of say Justin. Now it's my turn. The room's paid up until the weekend. After that, it'll be down to you. Bye."

He scrabbled at the covers, trying to drag them around his body as she turned her back on him. She closed the door firmly behind her, leaving him standing, open mouthed in the bedroom, unable to quite believe his ears.

The feeling of release, as she marched towards the lift, was unlike anything she had ever experienced before. Even when she and David had found out that they were to inherit over thirty million pounds each, and that they would never have to worry about money again, she had only felt a little out of her depth and slightly euphoric for a few weeks.

This feeling was entirely different. She wanted to clip her heels as she rode down in the lift. She wanted to shout, Hooray! Hooray! Hooray! To anyone who would listen to her. She giggled as she descended to the ground floor. She could hardly wait to telephone her brother and tell him she was free.

She said her goodbyes to the staff on duty, promising them that her early departure was none of their faults and assuring them that she would return soon. She walked out to the huge four by four that Justin had insisted they hire, and hoisted herself in. For a moment she felt slightly guilty at leaving him without transport, but then she shrugged. A rental company would deliver a car to the hotel if he rang them. She wondered what type of vehicle it would be, seeing that he would now be paying for it himself.

It was only as she put her hands on the steering wheel that she noticed her diamond engagement ring still sitting proudly on her left hand. She looked at it for a long moment and then slipped it from her finger. She squeezed it in her fist. There was no way she wanted to wear it any longer, but she certainly wasn't giving it back to Justin.

He hadn't bought it in the first place.

They had strolled along London's Bond Street together, a month after finding out that she had inherited a fortune, and then drifted into a wine bar for lunch. Justin had proposed to her over a delicious duck pate and then had made excuses for the fact that he hadn't bought a ring because he wanted her to choose something she liked. They had ended up returning along Bond Street and selecting a beautiful diamond cluster from Aspreys. She had been so excited that it taken another month for her to realize that Justin hadn't used his card to pay for it and he had never mentioned paying her back.

She could feel the stones pressing into her palm as she wondered what to do with it. She couldn't just chuck it out of the window in some grand gesture of her newly found freedom. It had cost a small fortune. She would sell it and buy something for her project with the proceeds. She slipped it into her pocket and felt another weight fall from her shoulders. At this rate she soon wouldn't need a car. She felt as though she could fly already.

She pulled out of the hotel car park and

drove slowly back down the road she had walked along the night before. She couldn't help but turn her head and stare into the thickness of the forest along the side of the road. There was no way she would have found her way through by herself. She wondered about the tall lopsided man for a few moments and then nearly crashed the car into the hedge on her side of the road as she saw him, a lone, dark figure standing just a few trees back in the woods. She saw him quite clearly, his pale features distinct against the trees, one side of his face covered with the long mop of dark hair.

She braked sharply and leapt out of the driving seat, leaving the door wide open and the engine running. She ran back a few paces and called out.

"Hey! You there! I've got your coat!" She was in no doubt at all that it was her rescuer, the scars she'd noticed the night before had been even clearer in the daylight. She jumped over the ditch at the side of the road, took a couple of paces into the undergrowth and then stopped as darkness closed in around her. She peered into the woods, surprised at their almost overwhelming thickness. All sounds of the nearby town seem to have been cut off as she entered the woods. They felt cold and unwelcoming. It was odd because she hadn't felt like this the night before with the man by her side. She shuddered as she peered into the gloom. The only sound was of the breeze drifting gently through the treetops.

The man had disappeared as silently as he had done the night before. She stood there feeling slightly ridiculous. Why had he ignored her, avoided her even? There was no way he hadn't seen her or heard her call. He had been staring right back at her as she had stopped the car, and if she had recognized him, then with his obviously superior eyesight, he would have easily recognized her.

"Hey! Essex boy! I only wanted to return your coat!" She called out a little more softly as she stepped backwards out of the gloom again. She shivered a little in the silence and then hopped back over the ditch. She walked quickly back to the open door of the car.

Perhaps he really hadn't seen or heard her, or perhaps he wasn't even the same guy. She must have mistaken shadows for scars because there was no reason at all why, if it had been her rescuer, he should ignore her. It was probably some other French chap out hunting. It was a common enough sport here in the countryside. She climbed back into the car and pulled the door closed behind her.

She took one last long look into the forest, staring hard into its impenetrable depths, hoping to catch another glimpse of his tall figure, and then she gave it up. She had an appointment to keep. She'd catch up with the man some other time and if she didn't, she'd leave his coat by the Chateau door. It seemed the obvious place. It would be a shame if she couldn't see him again. She wanted to find out if the strange electrical tingling that she had felt every time she thought about him was just a figment of her imagination. She flushed at the wild thoughts that came far too easily once again and pressed her hand to her belly to stop the mad flipping sensation deep in her stomach,

She lifted the bag holding his coat to her face and breathed the lush smell in deeply. Her stomach leapt again and her heart pounded furiously beneath her ribs. Oh God! She thought and closed her eyes. Why was she feeling like this when she was just sniffing at his old coat? Maybe it was just as well that she didn't meet him again. She didn't think her body could take it.

He had turned sharply away as soon as he realized who was in the giant car and that she had seen him. He had hurriedly stepped back deeper into the woods, and stood with his back pressed to the trunk of a wide pine tree, momentarily annoyed that he was going to have to delay his trip to the local market.

And then he took a quick glance to see if she was following him. His breath caught in his throat and he gazed at her, mesmerized, silent in his new hiding place. It hadn't been any trick of the moonlight. She was completely stunning. Her rich, chestnut hair was tumbling over her shoulders, sweeping across her beautiful face in the gentle breeze. Her eyes were the darkest brown, wide and framed by impossibly thick eyelashes. Her lips were full and tinged the softest pink. He groaned as he looked lower at her curving frame, fuller in exactly the right places and accentuated by a close fitting jumper and skin hugging jeans.

His stomach rumbled and clenched in tightly, but he didn't think it was because he was hungry. He waited quietly, hoping she would go away quickly, so that he could forget those wonderful curves and that beyond beautiful face. He needed to be practical and get to the market before it closed.

He had only just started plucking up the courage to limp along the stalls, buying meat and fish and delicious home grown vegetables. It had taken a week or two for him to notice that people didn't stare at him here. They didn't seem to mind his odd voice as he practiced his rasping, schoolboy French, ordering oddly named cheeses and strange cuts of meat. He had only found out later that they thought he was a leftover of an older era.

When he had bought his cottage in the

woods, all he had wanted was somewhere to live completely alone, where nobody could bother him ever again. He hadn't taken any notice of the fact that the tiny building stood in the grounds of the huge, derelict Chateau. He seemed to remember the agent telling him that the cottage had originally been the gardener's house, and that although it had no official garden itself, in an attempt to get someone to buy the place, it was being sold with access rights to the whole of the estate.

Estate was a very grand term for his overgrown surroundings. It might have once been a fabulous garden with acres of grounds, but now everything had been taken back by nature. The imposing driveway and avenue of trees were completely hidden already. There were remnants of the formal gardens, now being covered by the rampant rhododendrons and even though some of the remaining flowering shrubs looked good in the spring, they were fast being smothered by ivy and brambles.

The huge Chateau and stable block with riding school were also being suffocated by the relentless creeping growth. He kind of liked the abandoned look of the place. The empty windows, some with jagged broken glass still in their rotting frames, looked a little sad on a winter's day, but in the summer, they just begged to be peered through and investigated. The beautiful pale stone shone in the sunshine and the slipping slates on the roof gleamed dark purple in the moonlight.

When he had first moved into his cottage he was only glad that he had found somewhere perfect to live. Somewhere completely private, surrounded by dark woods that went perfectly with his black moods, but within a couple of weeks, he had been overcome with curiosity.

He had climbed through one of the broken windows and taken a look around the interior of the ruined Chateau. He had been surprised to find the huge cellar full of horribly familiar, old metal bed frames and stinking ruined mattresses. It hadn't taken him long to realize that the place had been used as some kind of hostel, almost like a hospital but not quite. Curiosity piqued, he had returned to the estate agent to enquire and had discovered that the original eighteenth century Chateau had been taken over during the Second World War by the invading German army, and then, when they had at last left, it had been used as a hospital and lastly a home for the mentally disturbed. That had closed in the late nineteen eighties and the place had been abandoned ever since.

A nut house! He had thought, not in the least bit alarmed. He was living in the grounds of the local mental asylum and the local residents had obviously assumed he was a relatively harmless madman.

He had laughed out loud at the discovery. No wonder his home had been so cheap. He was going to be surrounded by a load of lost nutters trying to find somewhere to sleep. He didn't mind. Sometimes he thought he was going to go completely mad himself. He thought he would fit right in.

But to his surprise, he hadn't been plagued by any unfortunate French madmen. Once or twice a few teenagers had come to have a bit of a rave in the ruined building. They lit small campfires and drank bottles of cheap French cider but they soon became bored of it all and they hadn't been back.

The estate agent had told him that the place would fall into complete ruin soon. It was too new to become a Historic Monument and therefore wouldn't attract government grants and it was going to be far too expensive to put the Chateau right unless someone wanted to make some sort of millionaire's playground type hotel out of it. It didn't seem likely. The north coast of Brittany had never really been on the millionaire's playground list and the original residents had all been taken very good care of elsewhere in the locality.

He'd been left alone, away from all the prying eyes, to wander around the place as much as he desired.

He pulled his leg over a fallen tree and thought of the beautiful young woman he'd just seen again. He had seen her fold the "For Sale" notice into her jacket the night before. It wouldn't be long before she turned up again. Hopefully she'd take one look at the place during daylight and scurry off back to the posh hotel from which she'd come. He hoped she'd remembered to put his coat in her enormous car and he hoped she would leave it for him. He certainly didn't want to have to ask for its return.

He had lain awake most of the night, strange and long forgotten stirrings, deep in his body denying him sleep. And now after he had glimpsed her a second time and heard her calling urgently, he knew he didn't want to see her again. He couldn't see her again. She was just too beautiful. It hurt his heart to see her, perfect and whole and deliciously fragrant.

He bit back the passions she had disturbed in him, and then laughed grimly at himself. There was no way it would ever come to anything. She had the super handsome boyfriend, he had noticed in the hotel, waiting for her. There was no way she would ever look at someone like himself. It was pathetic to even consider it. He shook the errant thoughts away as he raised his hand to his cheek and felt the hideous scars. He couldn't bear the thought of the look on her face if she ever saw him clearly. It would be more than he could stand to see her go screaming off into the distance when she saw him in the harsh light of day.

He flopped his long black hair back from his face and scanned back towards the road. The big car was gone. Thank God.

He limped out of the forest path and turned toward the town. His stomach rumbled loudly. This time it was definitely from hunger. He'd have to hurry before the market was all packed away for lunch, but the thought of fresh bread and all the delicious cheeses encouraged him to stride out, forcing him to swing his stiff leg forwards, ignoring the pain in his upper thigh as he half jumped, half staggered, across the ditch and into the road.

Chapter Four

Ellen parked the big car at the end of the market square. It was later than she had thought. The final argument with Justin and then stopping by the forest had held her up longer than she had expected. Stallholders were beginning to pack away their goods, but she could see the estate agency was still open across the square.

Anton Le Cam, the agency owner, had laughed when she had first telephoned that morning and mentioned the ruined Chateau. He had only stopped laughing when he realized there was a stony silence at the other end of the line. He tried to make excuses.

"…But it is a near ruin. It will cost you a fortune and never make a return. Why don't I show you some of the properties available at Plestin en Greve or at Loquirec? I'm sure they will be far more suitable. Your fiancé telephoned me yesterday and gave me all 'is requirements. I 'ave selected several places for you to view on the coast." There was more stony silence and then a voice so severe he could hardly believe it was the same person speaking.

Ellen could barely keep her irritation with Justin under control.

"Monsieur Le Cam, please understand that I am no longer associated with my ex-fiancé." She emphasized the ex. "I would be happier if you did not mention him again. I apologise if he misled you in any way, but my requirements are quite different from those previously explained to you. If you are not prepared to take me to the Chateau, I will have to go to the Maire, find out who owns the property and then go to them direct. They may be quite unhappy at the way you are not marketing their place to its best advantage."

There was a strangled grunt in reply and then she heard him let out a deep sigh.

"Non, actually they probably wouldn't care that much. It belongs to the commune, but as you seem very determined to visit, I will take you there. I will 'ave to make arrangements with the caretaker and then I'll 'ave to find you a 'ard 'at. I 'ave one 'ere somewhere but I loaned the other to Monsieur Reeves, but no matter, perhaps I can ask him to leave it for us. Why don't you come to my office in an 'our. I should 'ave made the arrangements by then. Oh, and I advise you to wear walking boots. I do not think I can get a car up the drive." He put the phone down sharply.

She couldn't really blame him for sounding so reticent. He was probably thinking the whole thing was a complete waste of his time.

She sat and played with her diamond clip as she watched the agent through the window of his office. She could see the man flapping his arms around wildly at a woman at another desk. She was pulling things out of a cupboard and suddenly turned around triumphantly as she pulled out a yellow hard hat. Le Cam stopped flapping and picked up his telephone again. She could see him start to flap again as he held a rapid conversation. His face began to turn red and then his shoulders slumped in defeat. He put the phone down slowly.

She could see him take a few calming breaths and then he picked up the telephone again. Her mobile rang on the seat beside her. His voice was a little hesitant.

She climbed out of his car as he began to speak to her.

"It is all arranged. We can go as soon as you arrive at my office, but I warn you, the caretaker is a little…'ow do you say?…Shy perhaps. 'e says 'e'll leave the 'ard 'at and the key by the door.

She was already halfway across the square as she replied.

"Shy? How is a caretaker shy? I would really like to see him and have his opinion on the place. I'd like as much information as possible." She dodged between the last of the market stalls being packed away.

Le Cam was apologetic.

"I will try again when we get there, but he is

a strange man. Very quiet. 'e won't like it if 'e thinks you are going to turn 'is Chateau into some sort of fancy 'otel." Anton Le Cam looked up as the phone clicked off. She pushed through the door of the agency and spoke directly to him returning her phone to her pocket.

"No, well I'm afraid that's his problem, but you can assure him I am not thinking of turning this into some sort of boutique hotel for the rich and famous. Peace and quiet is all that is required for my venture. Can you try to persuade him? I really would like his take on the place." She was running her fingers through her windswept hair, then she pulled the mass of dark curls over her shoulder, plaited it quickly and fastened it with her diamond clip.

Le Cam stared at her, his eyes wide, his mouth open in surprise. She was so young, but her demeanour was full of confidence. He came around her side of the desk, his arm outstretched in welcome. She was the most stunning woman he had ever seen. Everything about her, even her slightly muddy jeans and boots, gave an air of grace and beauty.

"Mademoiselle, please call me Anton. I 'ad no idea you were so nearby. Please come and sit while I find the papers for you to sign…a formality in case you go ahead with the purchase. But I am sure that you know all this." His accent was soft and warm.

She had a slim, old-fashioned fountain pen ready in her hand.

A few minutes later they were getting settled in his car. He apologized quickly as he swept paperwork and an old sandwich wrapper from the passenger seat, but she just smiled at him and told him not to worry.

They headed out of town along a narrow road. It twisted and turned taking them through the countryside before narrowing even further as the forest closed in, dark beside them. A few hundred meters on, they turned at a tight junction and then at the next corner a high wall separated them from the forest.

"This isn't the outer limit of the grounds." Anton nodded towards the wall. "The wall used to extend all the way to the ravine, but it 'as fallen in many places further along. This is the only part still standing. Take a look at the plans, there are tracks through the forest that take you across the river. You can see the estate includes that section of the river and all the fishing rights. There is also a small beach with mooring points further along."

He indicated over her shoulder and she reached back to pick up a folder. She opened it quickly and stared at the first picture. The whole estate was laid out on a Plan Cadastral. It was a vast area. She smiled as her eyes swept over the Plan. She looked carefully at the boundaries that almost bordered the town and the tracks that passed through it. She could see the one route crossing the river. It came out at Plestin, right on the edge of town. She turned over the page. There was an old black and white photograph, nearly sepia in colour now. It was of the front of the then majestic Chateau. Neatly dressed men and women wearing gleaming white aprons, stood self-consciously along the wide stone steps leading up to the front door.

Le Cam glanced at the picture.

"That was taken before the war. Just after the turn of the last century I believe, when the Chateau was still privately owned. All the old staff I think. Of course the place doesn't look like that now so please don't get too excited. I'm afraid you will be very disappointed." He stopped the car and pulled up onto the verge. She looked up from the photograph to see two huge stone pillars, draped in ivy and a mass of foliage between them. Le Cam looked at them ominously. "Maybe I should 'ave brought a machete.

Ellen laughed at him.

"Come on Anton, where's your sense of adventure? But are you sure this place has a caretaker? It doesn't look as if he does much caring."

He answered immediately almost defensive

at her tone.

" 'e's not really a caretaker. 'e bought the old gardener's cottage on the other side of the estate. Did you see it marked on the plan?" He waited while she leafed through the pages of the file again. She pointed to what were the stable blocks at the rear of the Chateau, but he swished her finger out of the way and tapped a much smaller rectangular image, more than half a kilometre away from the main house. "There! It is a little way from the main residence. Quite private. I sold the 'ouse to him. It 'ad been lived in more recently than the Chateau, but 'e has still 'ad to make a lot of renovations. Actually 'e is British like you. Ex-army man from what I see. 'e has been 'ere eighteen months or two years now, maybe and you should bear in mind that he 'as full access rights to all of the grounds including the river and beach. The Maire could not sell the place otherwise. You cannot change that agreement and that may not fit in with what you 'ave planned." He opened the car door and was about to step out when she laid her hand on his arm.

"You don't mean he is the man with the scars?" She waited for Anton to nod. "I have his coat." She patted the bag on her lap.

Anton raised his eyebrows, concern flitting across his face.

" 'is coat? 'ow? Did you find it? Was it

abandoned? I thought 'e sounded odd this morning. Is Patrick OK?"

She smiled at Anton's obvious disquiet and reassured him quickly.

"He seemed fine last night. No, it wasn't abandoned. He let me borrow it. I went for an unscheduled stroll on my way back from town last night. I had been viewing some properties with another agent, but they proved unsuitable. I wanted to get back to the hotel as quickly as possible and I thought the footpath would be a short cut, but I was very lost in the end. I discovered the Chateau and would have had to stay there the night if he hadn't come and rescued me. All this forest is very disorientating." She opened the car door and swung her slim legs out. Le Cam leapt from his side and rushed around to hold the door for her, but she was already closing it gently.

He stood for a moment and eyed her curiously.

"I wouldn't 'ave wanted to stay there all night." He shuddered theatrically and turned to search for their best way through the bushes.

"Why ever not? It wasn't a bit scary. I felt quite safe there actually." She peered through some ivy and spotted grey gravel a metre or two further ahead. "Here, I think. I can see what's left of the drive." She pushed through the undergrowth and found herself between an avenue of huge trees, overgrown but passable.

Le Cam joined her quickly.

"This place 'as too much 'istory. There are too many ghosts 'ere for me." He shuddered again. "Okay, now we 'ave found it, I think there is about 'alf a kilometre trek" He started off along the gravel.

She caught up with him quickly, suddenly more interested.

"Ghosts? Of whom? What do you mean Anton?"

He shrugged carelessly.

"There are stories of strange things 'ere. I don't know much about the goings on before 1940, but during the war the Germans were 'ere. They took over the Chateau, as they did with many of the great 'ouses in France. I don't know that this place was any worse than the others were, but it was a dark time for us, several young men from the town went missing. Screams were heard in the darkness and their bodies were never recovered." His voice was only just above a whisper. Then he cleared his throat. "And then afterwards it was used as an 'ospital of sorts. Many men came here with terrible wounds, either to recover or die." He looked over at her, but her expression was unreadable. "After that the...the unfortunate? I don't know the words. Well they came."

"Unfortunate? What do you mean?" She had stopped walking and was staring wide eyed at him now.

The estate agent turned to look directly at her.

"I don't know 'ow you say it...You know, odd." He twirled his finger at the side of his head.

"You mean mentally impaired?" Ellen was shocked.

Le Cam nodded vigorously.

"Yes! Yes, mental. That is the right word. Not particularly dangerous, you understand, just, well just mad or misunderstood perhaps. Of course, when the Chateau fell into bad disrepair, their 'ealth suffered and those that remained were moved out. It was too much for the commune to afford the repairs and the Maire made the decision to close it down. The last few patients are cared for in the villages now, but before then, all was not as good as it appeared."

Ellen pulled her jacket closely around her.

"Oh! Well I can understand that. Now-a-days we think of things like that slightly differently, thank goodness. But I haven't seen many people like that around here. Are you sure that you are talking of recently." She carried on walking smartly. It was Anton's turn to catch up.

"Well, not that recently, but then, by the

time it closed, there weren't that many of them left."
He whispered mysteriously.

Ellen stopped again and scrutinised his face carefully. She pressed her hands to her hips and shook her head as she caught sight of his mouth twitching at the corner.

"Anton!" She laughed. "You're trying to put me off! Why? You could gain an excellent fee."

He flushed at being found out so easily.

"Okay, I admit it. I don't know if there are ghosts, but the disappearances and other things are true. It's just that I like Patrick. We 'ave become good friends and 'e is a brave man. 'e has been dealt an unlucky 'and in life and I don't want to make it worse for 'im. When I sold 'im the gardeners cottage, I assured 'im that the Chateau was virtually worthless and would probably never be sold. I told 'im 'is 'ouse would be completely private. 'e is a very quiet soul and, I cannot lie to you, 'e doesn't want anybody else 'ere. I feel as though I am breaking my promise to 'im if you buy the place less than two years later." He shoved his way through the rhododendrons and they found themselves in the clearing in front of the Chateau.

Anton breathed a sigh of relief and looked up at the huge grey walls.

"Well, we 'ave arrived at last. Awful, isn't it? Do you really want to be bothered to look any further? I am sure I can find you somewhere else far more worth your while." He turned back down the driveway ready to leave, but stopped when he heard her brisk step tapping on solid stone. He turned back to see her running up the wide steps. She put the bag with Patrick's coat down as she moved nearer the walls.

"It's the most beautiful place I've ever seen." She was staring upwards at the old building, her expression rapt. The hazy sunshine was melting away the mist surrounding the Chateau and the pale stone shone through the moss and algae. She put her hand out to the wall and picked off some of the moss.

"It's limestone!" She exclaimed. Her fingertips were caressing the pale stone as if it could be soft.

Anton wandered up behind her and peered over her shoulder studying the stone intently.

"From Caen apparently. It is the same stone that was used in your Tower of London and St. Paul's Cathedral, the finest limestone in the 'ole world…The walls may be beautiful, but just look at the place, do you really want to go any further?" He craned his neck upwards. "The Maire 'ad quotes for renovating it a few years ago. The roof alone is going to cost over an 'undred thousand Euros and the window's, Mon Dieu! There are four floors. Look at them all, 'undreds of them and everyone will 'ave to be 'andmade. C'est impossible. C'est trop chere…it is going to run into millions before it will be complete, and then you 'ave the cost of furnishings and running the place. That is why the commune 'as never bothered. It is too much for the public purse."

"It's exactly what I'm looking for Anton. Can we go inside?" She breathed softly as though in awe of the majestic building.

Le Cam shrugged.

"I don't think that Patrick 'as been yet. I cannot see the 'at and we really shouldn't go inside without it." He started towards the front doors but it was obvious there was no hat. "Perhaps 'e is not yet returned from town. 'e said 'e was going to the market. I thought we would be longer getting 'ere. It might be better to wait in the car."

Ellen started to walk along the front of the building, peering in at each window as she passed.

"No, I don't want to go back. I don't mind waiting here. It's not cold."

Le Cam watched her as she walked away from him. She appeared to glide along the front of the Chateau, her hand outstretched, keeping contact with the stone. He spoke gently.

"'e may not come if 'e knows you are 'ere. I told you, 'e is very shy."

Ellen snorted.

"Well he certainly didn't appear at all shy last night. He more or less manhandled me back to the hotel."

Anton came up close behind her and placed his hand on her shoulder to stop her walking for a moment.

"But last night it was dark. I think it is more that 'e does not like people seeing 'im. 'is face is quite bad. Some people cannot 'ide their shock when they see 'im." His expression was gentle. It was quite obvious that he cared very much about Patrick's feelings. She was moved by his sensitivity.

She looked at the estate agent seriously.

"Believe me Anton, I really won't be bothered by what his face looks like. I'm absolutely sure it can't possibly be any worse than I've seen before. Give him a call and get him up here. Tell him I'm returning his coat. If he knows it's me he may not feel quite so worried." She sat down stubbornly on the balustrade that surrounded the walk.

Anton sighed and pulled his telephone from his pocket.

Patrick stared at her from the other side of the rhododendrons. They had arrived only a few moments before him and he'd been too late to leave the hat and key and get out of sight again. He'd remained hidden, hoping they would leave quickly, but as soon as he saw the way her hand moved gently across the stone walls, he knew it was hopeless. She looked completely in love with the place already. And when she'd sat down, he knew there would be no getting rid of her. He would have to show himself.

He shook himself defiantly. *What was the matter with him? He wasn't some idiot kid with a schoolboy crush.* He was thirty-two. Ex Special Services amongst other things. He had killed people. Lots of them, if he cared to count, which he didn't. They had all been worse than bad and deserved to die, so he wasn't going to worry himself over that. But here he was getting himself into a sweat, worrying over meeting this woman in daylight. *For God's sake! He had to get over this.* It wasn't as if he was some kind of ogre. Anton was his friend and he had overcome his fears for the market place, a mere slip of a girl shouldn't scare him.

He only wished that she weren't quite so beautiful. Last night he had thought that perhaps the moonlight was being kind to her, but after seeing her earlier as she jumped from her car, he knew it was no trick of the light. She was completely entrancing. The nearly forgotten passions began stirring again and he took a deep breath to calm them.

This was going to be harder than he had anticipated. He didn't want to see her expression when he finally limped into view. His phone buzzed in his pocket. He knew it was Anton, he could see the man with his own mobile pressed to his ear. He squared his shoulders, stood up as straight as possible and shoved forwards through the bush.

"Anton! I'm here. I was held up at the market." He called out as he revealed himself. He saw the woman's head come up and he stared hard at her, lifting his chin, challenging her and bracing himself as he waited for the shock to register.

He waited for her to drop her gaze. He waited for the fixed smile. He waited for her to be embarrassed, waited for the pity in her eyes…

Nothing…

Absolutely no reaction at all. She didn't bat an eyelid, merely stood up and came down the steps towards him, smiling a genuine smile that crinkled the outer edges of her beautiful brown eyes and sent sudden stabs of sharp pain into his heart. She bent to pick up a bag at the bottom of the steps and then walked right up to him.

"Hello again. I brought your coat. Sorry I rushed off with it last night, but thanks for the loan and thanks for taking me back to the hotel. I'm Ellen Phillips. From Essex." She finished, smiling up at him again. She hadn't realized how tall he was the night before. It had been so dark and they had been stooping beneath low branches and scrub. The tone of his voice hadn't told her much about his age either. Now she could see that he was probably in his early thirties, well over six feet tall, muscled and fit.

He stared down at her open gaze, his brows creased into a solid line of confusion.

Well, this was a new one on him. What the hell was the matter with her? Why wasn't she running for the hills? He lifted his hand to his face, wondering if, by some miracle, the disgusting hard, white skin was gone, then dropped it immediately as he touched the horrible numb, waxy texture. The scars were still there, the same as always, cold and terrible under his fingertips.

She was still looking at him directly, holding out a bag. Feeling a complete idiot, he reached out and took it from her. He looked briefly inside the bag and saw the thick lining of his coat. A wonderful delicate fragrance wafted up at him. Curiosity replaced his frown. He didn't think she could have worn it long enough for her scent to transfer. He hoped she hadn't sprayed it with perfume to mask the smell of his open fire. He looked right back at her.

"No problem, glad to have been of help. I'm Patrick Reeves, from Essex too, but you guessed that already. Thanks for bringing this back. Not that I need it so much, now that the weather is improving." He sucked in the words, feeling a complete fool for discussing the weather with someone so young and beautiful while desperately hoping that he wasn't dribbling from the scarred corner of his mouth. He lifted the back of his hand to check. No, it was dry, thank God!

She turned towards the Chateau.

"Did you manage to find the key? I'm dying for a look inside. I think it's going to be just what I want."

"Huh! You hardly need a key." He grunted doubtfully, as he looked down at her. "I think you might change your mind when you take a closer look. It's pretty bad."

He put the coat down on the balustrade and fumbled in his pocket, then limped up the stone steps. Now she did glance down, frowning as he walked past.

"Why do you still have one of the old models? Anton says you've been out here nearly two years. Have you been offered the new update?" She asked as he walked unevenly towards the Chateau door.

He stopped immediately.

"What? What do you mean?" He turned sharply, his dark blue eyes looked fiercely down at her and he dropped the key.

She raised her eyebrows in exasperation.

"Your leg of course. I wondered about it last

night. You're still using the old model. You're entitled to the new one. It has much improved ankle movement and uses a better suction cup at the top. More comfortable apparently. A lot less friction and a lot more mobility."

Patrick looked down at his leg. It was completely covered by his dark denim jeans and his brown boots were identical. How could she possibly know he had a prosthetic limb rather than just a limp? He looked harshly, accusingly at Anton but he just shook his head and shrugged.

He stooped to pick up the fallen key. His voice was stiff.

"I haven't got round to it, that's all. I haven't been back to the U.K since I bought the cottage and I've sort of got used to this one now." He was uncomfortable answering her question, but she didn't appear the least bit embarrassed, her eyes just grew wide in amazement.

"Well, you want to get yourself back there and get it sorted out. You can't let the government get away with making you put up with second best. You can always keep this one too but I would have thought it was quite restricting and it must be a pain in the ass to drag about in all this undergrowth." She indicated the bushes where he had been hiding.

He gawped at her incredulously, feeling the anger rise in him. *Who the hell did she think she was?* Preaching to him as though she would have any idea of what it was like to be blown apart and find your life completely ruined in less than a second.

He gritted his teeth before he spoke.

"I'll wear whatever type of leg I damn well like, thank you." He turned away from her sharply and growled over his shoulder. "Now do you want to see this place or not?" He held up the key and the hat.

She jogged up the steps behind him, completely unfazed by his angry tone.

"Yes please. Come on, you can take me round. Anton is afraid of the ghosts. Apparently there are the unhappy spirits of raging German despots, missing French prisoners, war wounded and displaced mad people." She counted them out on her fingers. "Should make for an interesting tour." She gave a pretend shiver as she grinned and lifted her chin towards Anton who was staring open mouthed at their exchange.

Patrick's furious tone disappeared immediately as he gazed incredulously towards Anton. He put his hands over his stomach and burst out laughing. The sound rang round the forest clearing and bounced off the walls of the Chateau.

"Ghosts! You're kidding me! Anton, really, is that the best you could come up with?" He shook his head as he calmed his laughter. "I should have thought that the dry rot was scarier."

Ellen looked up at Patrick in mock horror, noticing the deep blue eyes now sparkling under his dark hair. He was incredibly handsome. Even the vicious scars couldn't disguise his square jaw and generous mouth.

"Dry rot?" She gave a real shiver this time. "Now that really is scary. Lucky you came along Patrick. You don't look as though you would ever be scared of anything." She looked rather obviously across his broad shoulders and then down his wide chest to his slim waist, then even further to where she could just see the cup outlined below his muscled thigh. She raised her eyes again and felt herself blush as she realized that Patrick was staring right back at her, but her gaze still never faltered.

Patrick gawped at her. *Was she flirting with him? Impossible surely.* He turned away sharply, not wanting to see her embarrassment at being caught out, but then something made him turn back to her. His heartbeat quickened. She was still looking at him, not curiously, not with pity and certainly not afraid. She was just looking. Looking as though she liked what she saw. He felt his own face become hot under her open stare and his stomach gave an unexpected rumble. It sounded very loud in the stillness.

She looked down at his flat waistline again. And then, he could scarcely believe it, her dark eyes flicked even lower. His stomach rumbled yet again and she looked up at last, smiling widely at the sound. At least he hoped it was at the sound.

"Sorry. Have I made you late for lunch?"

He felt himself become even hotter as he beat down the violent surge of desire that had suddenly descended to his groin and he turned to shove his way through the great doors.

"No, more like breakfast actually. I went to the market to get bread and cheese, but I was delayed. My French is still a bit crappy." She was standing right beside him and he caught the hint of the same exotic perfume that had wafted up from his coat. He bent and picked up the hard hat and jammed it on her head. He limped forwards, pulling a flashlight from his pocket and shining it around in the darkness. She followed him into the vast open hallway.

"What about your hat? Anton has one outside for you."

He laughed grimly.

"Huh! What's the point? If anything falls on my head, it can't possibly do any more damage can it. Just mind where you tread." He stomped forwards, kicking a few shards of glass out of the way and she followed quickly. He shone his torch around in the gloom and she moved away from the shadows, closer to his shoulder.

She could smell the woodsy, herby, fragrance of him again and she breathed it in deeply. It was warm and delicious, safe and comforting. She leaned in closer, closing her eyes as she pulled in another long breath.

"Are you okay?" His voice was quizzical in the darkness beside her and she opened her eyes quickly as she realized how oddly she was behaving. He was staring down at her, his deep blue eyes just visible but his expression unreadable in the gloom.

She almost choked and her voice shook.

"Just a bit musty I think." She covered herself quickly, her heart pounding in her chest.

He sniffed loudly. All he could smell was her wonderful intoxicating fragrance. He tried not to notice it.

"Can't smell anything myself. Maybe it is the dry rot. I expect I'm more used to it." He made his tone indifferent though it was last thing he was feeling.

"Yes, you're probably right." She agreed. She closed her eyes once again. There was no smell of rot. It was him, his scent, his body. Her heart fluttered unevenly. She held herself as still as possible, trying to regain some sense of composure. And then she felt the air move gently as he walked away from her. She opened her eyes and stared at his tall figure. His broad shoulders moved fluidly, the muscles just visible beneath his shirt, his slim waist twisting gently as he made his way to the centre of the hall. She shivered all over, her whole body reacting to the overwhelming feeling of power that he exuded.

He spoke over his shoulder.

"Come on. We might as well go upstairs. We can only go to the first floor as after that it's mainly sky. You might as well see the worst of it first." He was already on the wide staircase and clomping up the first half dozen treads. He stopped when he didn't hear her follow.

He turned to see her staring at him again, her wide eyes travelling all over him, touching every inch of his body. Her lips were turned up at the corners. Not a full smile, just a look of…He didn't know what it was a look of. He looked at her curiously, then in astonishment.

It was a look of satisfaction.

That was the only way to describe it. She looked like a Cheshire Cat. The one that got a whole big bowl full of cream. He felt a strange thrill run through his body, flames of desire fuelling his whole frame.

And then he scowled at himself for being so stupid. It must be a trick of the light. She must just like the staircase or some other feature of the Chateau. There was nothing satisfactory about him to look at. Maybe a few years ago it might have been different, but not now. He cleared his throat, surprised at how dry it felt, and was about to speak when a shaft of sunlight shone through the still open doorway. Suddenly the whole hallway was lit up with thousands of sparkling lights.

It looked as though she were standing at the centre of her own universe, with a million stars held in her gravity.

"Wow!" He breathed quietly, as if not wanting to break some magical spell. "What the hell is doing that?" His eyes were darting this way and that, following the mass of twinkling sparkles. Then he stopped as he saw her radiant smile. It was brighter and more beautiful than any of the lights flashing about him. He gasped at her beauty, unable to take his eyes off her, and, shaking with emotions he hadn't dared to want ever again, he had to steady himself on the rotting handrail.

She smiled another breathtaking smile up at him.

"It's just my hairclip. Isn't it lovely? My brother gave it to me for my birthday. The stones are reflecting the light." She reached over her shoulder and pulled the end of her plait. The sparkling lights danced about the room as she twirled around, waggling the clip in the sunlight. They spun over the gloomy walls and danced on his denim clad legs as he stood on the stairs.

Patrick stood breathless, his heart hammering a frantic rhythm, the blood pounding through his veins.

And then she covered the clip with her hand. The room and his heart were plunged into darkness again.

Patrick blinked away the riotous emotions running through his whole being.

"Huh! Well at least you know what the place will look like if you turn it into a disco tech." He muttered frostily and was about to carry on up the stairs when he stopped. He turned to look back at her, suddenly curious, as she hurried to catch him up.

"How did you know about my leg? And how come you don't seem to notice my face?" His tone was almost accusing.

She jogged up the next couple of steps to stand beside him. She smiled radiantly again and gazed, unafraid, into his blue eyes as she scoffed.

"Of course I noticed it. I'm not blind." She was completely unembarrassed. "My brother had both of his legs blown off three years ago in Afghanistan, along with most of his face. If he hadn't had the best body armour, he would have been killed. Some fourteen year old kid had been persuaded to become a suicide bomber. Terrible thing to make a child do. I guessed something like that had happened to you too. You look kind of the same as David but not so…well, not so bad, but of course, I don't mean bad, because David doesn't look bad. He just looks like David now and not David before. I didn't know what you looked like before, so you just look like you to me. And just so you know, I think you look great actually. Does that make sense?" She looked up at him, her face twisted as though she were thinking hard.

Patrick stared at her in complete amazement. She was so open. He had never heard anybody describe him like that since the bomb. He had avoided people so much, he rather hoped they wouldn't be able to describe him at all. He shook his head.

"Huh! No not really. My face looks like shit, and the rest of my body is loathsome. If your brother got hit worse than me, I feel sorry for him." He stomped up the last flight of stairs, leaving her trailing behind him.

She was silent as she tried to catch him up. She couldn't fathom his mood swings. One second he seemed light hearted and happy and the next a bewildering hulk of glowering hardness. The anger was rolling out of him at that moment, but it didn't seem to be directed at her. Perhaps it was at himself.

It was impossible to guess.

They reached the upper floor and he guided her through the rooms to the front of the Chateau. He delighted in showing her the curl of smoke, wafting through the forest, from his own chimney, and the break in the tall trees at the head of the ravine. Then he stomped furiously back along the gallery to the staircase, begrudgingly taking her back down stairs, through the great hall again and round to the back stairs and the cellar.

She ignored his wavering moods. She was happy just to be in his presence. Every time his deep voice growled at her in the dim light, her whole body shivered in delight. Several times his hand brushed her arm and heat burned through the fabric of her jumper. She breathed in his wonderful manly scent and kept as close to him as possible.

The cellar was pitch black. Patrick shone the flashlight over the damp, grimy walls. At some point in time they had been covered in wildly extravagant wallpaper. Now it hung limp and mouldering, peeling away from the plaster and falling onto the tiled floor.

She kicked a curling sheet out of their path.

"Ghastly pattern. I can't imagine having to look at that all day." She murmured as they passed through a long corridor with rooms off each side. He shone the torch briefly into each room. Some were bigger than others. She walked into one that appeared to have a small window at the top of the outside wall. She reached up, rubbed away the festoon of cobwebs, and peered out. She could see a pair of legs swinging on the wall outside, feet kicking at the gravel.

"Not much of a view either." She giggled as Anton dragged his toe in the dirt and swore flamboyantly in French at the scuff on his shoe. She glanced back into the room and then outside again. "I wonder what these rooms were used for. They're so dark and if they had bars they'd look almost like prison cells."

Patrick came into the room behind her and stood looking down at her. Her face was still tilted up towards the slither of daylight. Her skin looked almost luminescent in the soft light.

There was a cobweb falling from her hat across her forehead. He pulled the hat from her head and placed it on the windowsill, then he reached up a finger to lift the thick web from her hair and face. His fingertip touched her skin on her forehead. She didn't flinch. She just stared back up at him, her eyes wide and sparkling.

He could barely breathe, the air felt almost thick in his lungs. He pulled back a fraction, needing some distance, and dropped his hand to his side.

"I think they must have been dormitories

from when the place was a mental home or maybe treatment rooms. I came down here once before. There are old bed frames and mattresses in some of the other rooms. All rotten and pretty uncomfortable looking. I wouldn't have fancied being shut up in here." His voice was soft again, almost a whisper.

She lifted a pale hand to his wide shoulder and brushed gently at his thick cotton shirt.

"No, me either, must have been awful..." She hesitated for just a moment and then carried on. "You have cobwebs on you too." She said gently as her hand came up to the unscarred side of his face and she wiped her thumb lightly across his cheekbone. She was very close to him, her breath cool and sweet.

He stood very still, his hands clenched tightly at his sides as her fingertips touched his skin. His heart was crashing against his ribcage, his blood racing through his veins so fast he could hear a rushing noise in his ears. He couldn't stop himself. He lifted his hand again and touched her plaited hair.

His voice sounded as soft as the gossamer threads wafting in the air around them.

"They get everywhere. This place hasn't been cleaned for years." He ran his fingertips over the side of her face, feeling the contours of her cheekbones as fire leapt through his body at her tender warmth.

She hadn't moved away from his touch. She hadn't moved at all. She was still staring up at him. He could hear her fast, shallow breaths. Her lips were just parted over her teeth and he could see them glisten moistly. Her top lip quivered a fraction, just a tiny, involuntary flicker.

Realization suddenly flooded over him. His whole body leapt with anticipation. She wanted this. She wanted him to kiss her. Her desperation was almost as acute as his own. He bent his head, completely unable to resist, wanting to taste her more than anything in the whole world. Her rose coloured lips were just a whisper from his, warm and succulent, trembling with desire. He could feel their heat, could taste her delicious breath in his mouth, he hesitated for a second longer wanting to prolong this moment, this torture, wanting it to last as long as possible. Her eyelids closed slowly. He breathed a deep sigh of longing, shut his own eyes and bent even further, his lips brushing the outer corner of her beautiful mouth.

There was a loud crack as the pane of glass above them shattered and his eyes flew back open.

A small stone clattered to the floor between them and Ellen jumped back in surprise. She looked as though she was going to faint. Patrick leapt forwards to catch her, but she swivelled out of his arms towards the broken window.

"God Anton! Be careful, you nearly hit us."
She shouted up through the small hole in the glass.

There was a mumbled response and then more grating on stones. Anton's face appeared at the tiny window. He knelt down and squinted at the broken window then peered around in the gloom.

"Mon Dieu! What an 'orrible place. All those spider webs, ugh! They must be monstrous, crawling creatures. You must come out now Patrick, whatever are you thinking of, taking a lady into such a disgusting cave? Are you nearly done? It's getting very late for lunch." He was backing up, moving away from the window as he dusted his knees.

Patrick glanced back towards Ellen. She was looking down at herself, brushing more cobwebs from her jacket. Even in the dark, he could make out the deep flush on her cheek. She was obviously embarrassed now. What on earth had he been thinking? She didn't want to be kissed by him, what beautiful woman would? He must have been delusional. He aimed his voice towards the window.

"We'll be about five minutes Anton. We're all but done here now." His tone was harsh and then he was silent.

Ellen stopped brushing her jacket and looked up at him in the gloom. Her pulse was still racing in her body, but she felt a cold shiver as she watched his face. His eyes had been burning with desire, but now they were as cold as ice. His lips had been as soft as melted chocolate, but now they were as firm as set concrete. His shoulders had been surrounding her, deep and caressing, enclosing her in warmth and security, but in less than a second everything had changed. He was as stiff and unyielding as granite. She couldn't fathom his expression at all. She must have been mistaken his intensions. Her imagination was running wild. Maybe he hadn't been about to kiss her at all, he was just getting the cobwebs out of her hair. That was what she had felt brush over her lips, just a silken cobweb. She blushed even deeper at her error.

"It's filthy down here. Let's move on shall we?" There was a strange tremble in her tone.

He was silent for a breath longer, then his eyebrows came together in a stiff line.

"Yes let's. There are only a couple more rooms to see." He was marching out of the room even before she could reply.

They clambered over the rotting mattresses and between the old metal bed frames. Her nose crinkled up at them in disgust. She looked so beautiful, for a moment he lost all concentration. His false leg hit an old bed frame. He stumbled for a second, and she caught his arm before he fell. He shrugged her off angrily, completely bewildered by the emotions running through him, and for a second she cowered back from his furious expression. Instantly he felt appalled. For the first time a reaction from her had wounded him. But it was nothing that she had done. His heart plunged to his stomach. He had frightened her at last, but with his anger not his looks. A terrible guilt consumed him. He tried not to look at her again.

They stumbled back up the stairs, into the light.

Anton was lying along the balustrade, Patrick's coat bundled up under his head, his eyes closed. He looked comfortable in the sunshine.

Still slightly breathless, Ellen prodded him on the shoulder and his eyes flicked open immediately.

"At last you are 'ere again, I 'ad no idea we would be this long. Now can we go?" He was impatient to be gone.

Ellen put a hand on his shoulder stopping him from darting back down the overgrown path to the car.

"Just a moment Anton. I think the Chateau will be perfect for me. It's a blank canvas. I can do exactly what I need. Have you had any offers for it?" She asked and out of the corner of her eye she saw Patrick's shoulders slump in defeat.

Anton looked up at the sky and laughed out loud.

"You must be joking. Monsieur Patrick 'ere, 'as been the only one near the place for years. As I said before, it is too expensive for most people to renovate, not that it means you can come in with a silly offer if you are truly keen. The Maire needs the money raised for other projects in the area. 'e won't let it go for nothing. And 'e will need to see proof that you have some kind of secured finances, something from the bank perhaps, before 'e will let the place go. 'e won't want you to buy it and then not do anything with it."

Ellen smiled at him and patted his arm. At least it would be easy to reassure him on that score.

"Let's go and talk some figures Anton. Perhaps we can come to some agreement. I want to speak to my brother too. He'll be working on the project with me as soon as he can get here."

She looked back at Patrick. He was closing the doors and turning the key once again. He handed it to Anton and lugged his coat out from under Anton's head. His expression was grim. He didn't look at Ellen.

"I'll leave the key with you. And if you don't need me anymore, I'm going to cook my lunch." He didn't wait for a reply, but folded up his coat and stamped off towards the forest.

Ellen called after him.

"Thanks for showing me around. I'll look

forward to being your neighbour."

Patrick spun back to her, his face aghast at the prospect. He couldn't have her anywhere near him. She was too beautiful and too fragrant and too irrepressible and the hour spent with her in such close proximity had been almost unbearable. He had wanted to kiss her so desperately. His anticipation had been at such a height, he had wanted to do a lot more than kiss her. His passion had been so great, so hard, that if she had given him the slightest encouragement he would have taken her there and then, ripping his clothes from his body before tearing hers aside and then making love to her on the filthy floor of the cellar.

But he had completely misunderstood her body language. That had been obvious when she had suggested they move on. She was just too polite to tell him outright that his ruined face and body didn't mean a thing to her. He wanted to kick himself for his own stupidity. He should have known what she would be like. He'd lived in Colchester for long enough. Her friendly, flirty openness, when she was with him, meant nothing. It was all just an Essex girl's facade.

His blood pounded, raging through his veins as he glared at her, hating her for making him feel a complete fool. Pain made him snarl the words.

"My neighbour! Not if I have anything to do

with it, you won't. Let's get one thing straight right now. I bought my place on the understanding that I was going to be left alone. If you think you're going to turn this place into some fancy hotel, with hundreds of rowdy guests running all over the forest, then I'm sorry, but I will be objecting. There's a hotel nearby already. If you remember, you stayed there last night. With a bit of luck they won't want you here either." And with that he shoved the bushes savagely and disappeared back into the woods.

Chapter Five

It was hers.

She was so excited that she couldn't not stay there. She spent the first day making one of the downstairs rooms habitable. She swept the floorboards and rigged up some material at the broken windows. She breathed a sigh of relief as she heard the weather forecast that promised it would be dry for the next week and she threw down her camping gear. Then unable to bear waiting to employ professional gardeners she spent the first backbreaking few days hacking away at the overgrown driveway, keeping a constantly burning bonfire to consume the detritus.

Each night she lit oil lamps around her makeshift bedroom and ate bread and cheese bought at the local market. She washed in bottled water and drank glasses of sparkling wine in the lamp light. Every night she fell exhausted into her sleeping bag and each morning she was out early, dragging the ivy away from the tall avenue of trees and clipping brambles away from the rhododendrons. By the end of the week she had discovered where to find the water main and the next day she rigged up a garden hose in the stable block. She shrieked and laughed as she took her first freezing cold shower.

Buying the Chateau hadn't been a problem

at all. The negotiations over the price had been more like haggling over a second hand car, than an eighteenth century building. The paperwork was hurried through and the Maire had looked very happy at the bargain.

Clearing the place completely was first on the agenda and then putting in some form of electricity. She watched in satisfaction as the first lorry drove up the newly cleared driveway and deposited a huge skip. She directed her workmen to the basement first.

The cellar was the least damaged area of the property. The workmen soon removed all the old beds and reeking mattresses before moving on to the upper floors while Ellen carried on with the planning of the basement pool and luxury treatment rooms.

She wanted to keep as many of the original features as possible and was pleased that the eighteenth century tiling was still in place in many of the rooms. Some of the rooms in the cellar only needed new wiring and then decorating. She tackled the room where Patrick had almost kissed her, herself. After the glazier had replaced the broken window, she brushed the cobwebs from the ceiling and cleared the debris and filth of years from the tiled floor.

She stood and stared out of the now clean window, her heart racing as she thought of how close she and Patrick had been, of how his fingers had touched her face. She closed her eyes and tried to imagine him there with her now. Her breath came in uneven gasps as the feelings grew in her. Her body began to tremble. A terrible wave of desire swept over her.

She hadn't seen him since that day. She wanted him with her now.

There was a small cough behind her. Her eyes flew open as she spun towards the sound.

"Patrick! You came back!" Her delighted exclamation immediately died on her lips as the man standing in the doorframe stepped forwards into the room.

"God Ellen, it's only been a few weeks. Surely you can't have forgotten my name already?" Justin stepped over the pile of dirt she had swept and walked across the room.

Ellen stood stiffly, the broom held defensively in front of her, her hands resting on the top of the handle.

"What are you doing here Justin? How did you know where to find me?" Her tone was not welcoming.

Justin flipped dust from the shoulder of his expensively tailored suit.

"You don't need to sound quite so pleased to see me." He said sarcastically. "I saw David a couple of weeks ago at an army do. He told me that you had bought this place. It was more difficult to find than I had imagined. It's not on any of the maps. I had to ask for directions from some sort of hobo who lives in the woods around here. You should be careful. Horrible character, dangerous looking, nearly as bad as your David, lame and ugly as sin, covered in scars."

Ellen drew in a furious breath.

"How dare you talk about David and Patrick like that! They can't help the way they look. And Patrick happens to be a very nice man anyway. He's not dangerous at all." She bristled instantly in Patrick's defence.

Justin threw his head back and laughed. The sound echoed wickedly around the room.

"Oh I see, that's why you called out Patrick when I arrived. You haven't changed much Ellen, still a sucker for a good sob story. So you're enjoying a bit of rough are you? Well, I hope he finds you more fun in bed than I did."

Ellen ignored his remark, not wanting to be reminded that she had slept with Justin for several years. She shivered in self-disgust. She didn't want to prolong the conversation any more than she had to.

"What do you want here anyway Justin? I have a lot to do as you can see, so unless it's very important, please don't waste any more of my time than you have to." She was as dismissive as possible.

Justin whistled through his teeth as he sauntered further into the room.

"When I saw David he was so over the top about this place. He was full of it. I thought you might need a business manager. You know, someone who really knows how to run things. Someone with plenty of experience." He was peering up through the window. "Hmm, nice view." He added sarcastically as he watched a pair of workman's boots march past.

Ellen's mouth had fallen open at his arrogance. She closed it quickly.

"And just what sort of experience do you think you've got Justin?"

He turned and smiled lazily at her.

"Oh you know. All those places in Spain. I've done a fantastic deal on them and sold the lot for twice what we paid."

She raised her eyebrows in surprise.

"Oh really? What I paid you mean. And just how did you manage to sell them when the papers transferring ownership haven't even been signed off yet? They're still at my solicitors." She began walking towards the door wanting to be out of the confined space.

He caught hold of her arm as she passed

him. He held it tightly, his thumb digging into her flesh and bruising her skin.

"Well, that's another of the reasons I came to see you. I couldn't miss out on the deal and so I signed on your behalf. The only problem is now that you will get half of the money. I was thinking that you would hand that over to me."

Ellen shook her head in amazement.

"You signed on my behalf? How?" She didn't wait for a response. "You mean you forged my signature? You fool Justin! Why couldn't you wait? If I chose to, I could call in the fraud squad and then you wouldn't get a penny."

He pulled her arm and dragged her close to him. She could smell his sour, greedy breath.

He leered down at her.

"But you're not going to do that are you? You're going to get your cheque book right now and hand me the money." His tone was full of menace.

She wrenched her arm away from him, not caring if she made the bruising worse, and glared up at him.

"When the money arrives in my account I will deduct any expenses you may have incurred on my behalf and then I'll give the difference to charity. You can keep your half and I won't get the police involved. How about that for a bargain? Now get out!" She stood by the door, quivering with rage.

She turned her face away as Justin crowded in on her, breathing heavily over her.

"You bitch! I'll leave when I'm ready. And I'm not ready yet. If you're not willing to give me my money, perhaps you'd be willing to give me something else. Something a little more personal. You like it rough, so how about a little rough with me, here, right now. I'm sure you'll enjoy it and at least I don't look like I've been through a mincing machine." He reached out and was about to pull her back towards him when she spun away from his grasp. Her plaited hair flew round her face and her diamond clip caught him on his chin.

He gasped in pain and put the back of his hand against his face. His hand came away smeared with blood. He glared at her furiously, dangerously.

"That bloody hair clip! You wear the damned thing all the time. You're a multi-millionaire and you can't even be bothered to go and buy something half decent. You're a sentimental fool and only wear it to keep that cripple of a brother on your side. I don't know why you bother, he's as useless as that clip."

Ellen took a deep breath. She was furious but she was also afraid as she watched a drop of blood ooze from the cut and run down his chin.

"I'm sorry Justin. I didn't mean to hurt you. Maybe I will reconsider the money, but I really can't do anything about it until I receive my share. Nearly everything I have is tied up here. Even you must see that. Now I really would like you to leave. I am very busy." She hoped to placate him long enough for her to get out of the cellar.

For a moment he looked as though he was going to argue, but just then limping, uneven footsteps could be heard echoing along the corridor.

"Ellen?" The voice came from nearby. "Ellen? Are you here? Did he find you?"

Ellen felt her breath rush from her body.

"Patrick! Yes, I'm fine. Justin was just leaving." The relief was audible in her tone.

Justin looked out into the corridor and came face to face with a glaring Patrick. He mumbled a few words about feeling claustrophobic and then pushed past. His feet could be heard clattering up the steps of the cellar.

Ellen stumbled towards Patrick. She was about to throw her arms around him when she stopped suddenly. He was glaring down at her now, his eyebrows furrowed, his mouth set in a grim line.

"He asked me the way. I didn't know if he had found you. The workmen told me you were down here…" He was silent for a second.

Ellen gulped back tears of relief.

"Patrick! Thank God you came. He was…" She didn't finish. Her breath was coming in panicked gasps.

Patrick glowered down at her still, his dark blue eyes glittering in anger.

"You never said that you were engaged." His voice was accusing.

She blinked in shock and stepped back.

"I didn't think I had to say. I never got the chance. You stormed off the last time I saw you. And anyway, I'm not eng…" She didn't have the opportunity to finish.

He flung up a hand, waving her words away.

"I don't want to know. I only came to make sure your fiancé had found his way." He interrupted bitterly and turned quickly not wanting to see her face properly.

"Patrick! He's not my…" But he was already making for the stairs. "Oh what's the point, if you're not going to listen anyway." She finished lamely and she turned back to the room and continued with the sweeping.

The clearing took over two weeks, skips arrived empty and were taken away overflowing with rotting debris. Then scaffolding went up, cloaking the beautiful building in a web of grey steel. Another month was spent stripping the place down and conserving anything that could be saved.

A specialist team came in to flood the walls and the remaining wood with rot and insect treatment and Ellen worked for days with an architect, putting down all her ideas on paper and letting him turn them into fabulously detailed drawings. She sent another team of workers to the stable block and riding school to start renovations there.

She poured over the French permit forms, asking the local workmen for advice when she didn't understand a question, while she wished she had taken more notice of her French teacher at school. Construction certificates were at last written up and lorry loads of wood and tiles arrived daily.

The roofers came in to replace the missing turrets and tilers began on the slates. The Chateau rang with the sound of hard work.

Ellen didn't see Patrick again.

She knew he was about, she could smell his wood fire every morning and she sometimes thought she caught sight of him prowling through the undergrowth. Several times she tried to call on him, wanting to keep him appraised of her plans, her heart pounding as she made her way to his door, but he was either out or ignoring her because he didn't respond to her knocking. Each time she trudged miserably back to the Chateau, the ache in her chest thudding dully.

She tried to put all her thoughts of him to

the back of her mind. She couldn't become so involved or so distracted. It was obvious he wasn't interested. She felt awful at upsetting his peace and quiet, but there was no other way to proceed. If he was going to avoid all contact with her, there wasn't a lot she could do. It wasn't as though she could go barging into his house unasked, although she very much wanted to.

Her next big hurdle was the permission for a change of use to a hotel. There had been several objections to her proposal, although nobody had seen her final plans, and because they could affect the town considerably, a meeting had been arranged in the town hall. Anton had told her that there would be a lot of interest from many townsfolk. On her side, the Maire was all for anything that would bring the prospect of more jobs and visitors to the area, but many were against the whole idea, preferring the peace and quiet to which the town was accustomed.

She woke on the morning of the meeting with a nervous flutter in her stomach.

Ellen was going to unveil her finalized plans that afternoon. She had been hoping to see Patrick the evening before the meeting to go over her ideas and reassure him, but he had avoided her yet again and she had stomped home, furious at his stubborn refusal to see her.

She climbed out of her sleeping bag, stiff and un-rested. The sun was in full force now June had arrived and the morning was already hot. She straightened her sleeping bag on the floor and rolled her shoulders. She hadn't slept properly in weeks and she was beyond tired, her body aching from sleeping for months on the hard floor.

After the first week of clearing, she had been intending to sleep at the local hotel, but when it became obvious that the owners were unhappy about possible competition, she had just slung a bedding roll on the floor of one of the better rooms and had made it her makeshift bedroom.

She grabbed the only dress she had brought with her from her suitcase and walked through the hall.

She slipped into the kitchen and washed in the huge sink. It was inconvenient and still only ran with cold water, but she was waiting for the plumbers to arrive. They were due in a few days time as soon as her permits were in place. She could barely wait for her first hot shower. She brushed her hair and tied it back using David's diamond clip hoping it would bring her good luck. Then she slipped the pale yellow dress on quickly and turned the kettle on.

She unrolled the plans and sat with her tea going over and over them, making sure she had answers to every possible question and contingency plans if she didn't.

She lifted her head and looked through the window as she heard a truck pulling up outside. She was surprised to see Monsieur Sylvan arriving with his lorry. Now the windows had arrived and been fitted perhaps the ugly grey scaffolding was being removed at last. She walked outside to see the work wondering why he was three days early.

She waved at the driver of the truck and he sprang out of the cab to greet her.

"Mademoiselle, a good day for you I think and for me too. Your workers 'ave finished just in time. I 'ave to get this all removed and on the truck by tonight. Another job 'as come up. A superb opportunity, the men are very 'appy to 'ave more work confirmed, but I 'ave to be on site first thing in the morning or I will lose the contract. 'ave you anyone 'ere that can help me load up today?"

Ellen shook her head.

"Today? No, everyone has the day off. I'm going to the town hall. There is the meeting arranged for the change of use. I thought we had an agreement that this lot would be staying until the end of the week?" She put her cup on the windowsill and looked around the Chateau. There were no other workmen here today. She had given them all the day off because she was going to be at the planning meeting and many of them wanted to see how it would all go down with the locals. "I don't have anyone here today Monsieur Sylvan. I wasn't expecting to have this lot loaded quite that soon."

Monsieur Sylvan gave an expansive shrug.

"But I must 'ave it all by the morning regardless, or I will lose a great deal of money and my men will 'ave no work. I will 'ave to charge you if it is not loaded in time."

Ellen looked taken aback at his tone. There was no way he was going to make her pay for his change of plans.

"Then I will have to deduct your daily rate for the three days that you agreed to leave the scaffolding here. I can work that out quite easily. But whether I can adjust your fees or not I'm certainly not going to be able to get that lot loaded by tonight, I just don't have the workforce and it's too late to get them to come in now."

Monsieur Sylvan shook his head and frowned.

"Maybe you do not understand me. I 'ave to 'ave it done by the morning. The loss of the contract will leave me thousands out of pocket. I'm not prepared to lose that kind of money. And my men, they will be furious if they 'ave no job. I really don't want to 'ave to charge you extra." He puffed out his chest.

Ellen didn't want to argue. She was simply too tired and today's meeting was too important to risk confrontation. She couldn't face the whole of the town having just had a dispute with one of its most respected tradesmen.

"Look, I do understand, but it's not my fault if you confirmed a contract that you can't fulfill. I have an agreement with you that I hire your equipment until the end of the week. That's what I've paid for. I don't want you to lose the opportunity of more work but I just can't see how I can help you. Isn't there some way round this?" She thought hard as Monsieur Sylvan puffed his cheeks and pursed his lips. Ellen carried on. "I mean, do you need all of the scaffolding by the morning? Can you make do with just some of it and then come back for the rest another day? Surely so long as you are on the next site and making a start, no one would object." She was pleading to his better nature.

He thought for a few seconds and then looked at the truck again. He turned towards her with a small smile.

"As it is you Mademoiselle, I think I could make do with about 'alf. It is only because you have used all my stocks of scaffold. This is such an 'uge 'ouse, but maybe I will get my men to take the whole lot down today. They will take one load, if you can get a second next truck loaded by eight in the morning then I will come back for the last of it Thursday. Can we agree on that?"

Ellen looked at the vast amount of metal pipe and scaffold boards. It would be a mammoth task but she couldn't see any other way round the problem. She nodded in agreement, as there was nothing else she could do.

"I'll do my best. And now I have to go. I have a meeting this afternoon with the Maire and I must have everything prepared. I can't be late. I'll see you at ten in the morning." She was buying herself another couple of hours loading time. She didn't have a clue of how she was going to load a whole lorry by herself, but as she had nobody else to rely on, she would have to try. Maybe she could get a couple of the plumbers to help her in the morning. They seemed to be fit enough for the task but she had long since learned that the French workers were only prepared to do their own job and refused to interfere with any other. It just wasn't done.

She returned to the Chateau and gathered up the plans and paperwork she needed for her presentation, and jumped into her tiny Fiat.

The Maire greeted her at the town hall, like an old friend, kissing her on both cheeks. He showed her to a chair on the raised dais at the front of the rows of chairs.

She was shocked at the amount of seats that

had been put out. She had had no idea that so many people were interested in her plans and she became even more worried as the seats began to fill quickly. She kept her head down and tried not to make eye contact with anyone, but it was harder than she thought. People seemed to be ranging themselves into two groups, those for and those against. The numbers looked to be in her favour, but in the growing crowd it was impossible to tell. She saw Anton Le Cam arrive and sit himself right at the back of the hall with the people she thought were against her plans. He smiled up at her apologetically. She smiled back at him. She didn't mind his apparent disloyalty. She knew he was here for Patrick.

And then, just as the hall looked to be full to bursting point, Patrick himself limped in. She saw several people glance nervously over at him and then move their eyes away quickly.

Her heart leapt into her mouth and her throat felt dry. She had longed to see him for weeks, but not under these circumstances. She gazed at his lean face, trying to keep her breathing under control.

His hair was longer than the last time she had seen him and his face appeared thinner, his dark blue eyes sought hers and just for a second she thought he was going to smile at her but then he pulled his eyebrows together fiercely and sat down next to Anton.

Her gaze dropped to the papers in front of her and she barely heard a word as the Maire called the meeting to order and began to outline her plans.

For a few moments after his initial address there was stunned silence and then suddenly murmuring broke out around the whole hall. She dared to look up to see if Patrick had been swayed in any way, but his seat was empty now. It was obvious that he had left before the end of the presentation.

The Maire invited the people to ask questions and although a translator was available, she answered them, in her improving but faltering French, as fully as she could. An hour later she was standing in the sunshine outside the town hall with all her permissions signed, sealed and delivered.

Several people came up to her and shook her hand. One elderly man cried openly in front of her, his arms waving as he gabbled on in rapid French reminiscing about the Second World War and then he kissed her several times on each cheek.

"I told you there would be nothing to worry about." The Maire was beaming at her, patting her arm with genial familiarity. "It will be a privilege to have all your guests come to our town. They will be welcomed by every citizen. France would no longer be free if the British had not come to our aid. All of our soldiers have been forgotten for too long. I don't know why your idea hasn't been thought of before."

"Perhaps I have more reasons than most to think about it Monsieur, but I really must be going. I have to go and see Mr. Reeves and get him to sign these papers, then I can make a proper start on the project." Ellen slid through the gossiping crowd and walked back to her car.

She drove slowly back to the Chateau, peering through the trees, hoping to catch a glimpse of Patrick as he made his way home. She was so tired, the day had been more stressful than she would have believed possible. She was more than relieved as she drove between the gateposts of the driveway, she could barely stay awake, but as she arrived at the end of the avenue of trees, her eyes opened wide in horror.

There was a mammoth pile of metal piping and a huge stack of wooden boards lying in front of the Chateau. In her euphoria at having the plans passed she had forgotten about Sylvan's scaffolding.

She knew there had been a lot of it, at least four loads had been delivered when the work had started, but when it was all up around the building it didn't look as nearly much as the mountainous heap that lay before her. It was going to take her hours, if not days, to get it even half loaded. She manoeuvred her car around the open backed lorry that stood hopefully beside the metal piping and parked the car at the back of the Chateau. She groaned as she looked back at the pile of metal. It was no good worrying about it. It would have to wait a little longer. She had to see Patrick first.

She trudged through the forest to his cottage, wondering if she would be able to break the door down if he refused to answer her this time, but she was amazed to discover that the door was wide open.

"Patrick" She called softly. "Can I talk with you?" She put her head around the frame. She breathed deeply with relief and her heart fluttered madly as she saw him standing with his back turned towards her. He poured water from his kettle into a mug.

He lifted his head at her words, but he didn't respond verbally or turn around.

She was hesitant, not wanting him to turn her out.

"I've brought some papers for you to sign. I was going to give them to you after the meeting, but you left early." She said quietly, her heart hammering with more nerves than she had experienced at the town hall. "Shall I leave them here on the table?" His silence was worse than an angry outburst. "Please Patrick." She begged. "Don't ignore me. The papers are official, you will have your own area of land right around your house. No one will be allowed to enter without your permission. You can still have your privacy."

He banged the kettle back onto the stove and answered her at last, his voice tight with anger.

"I have rights, you know. You can't keep me out of the estate. Don't think you can buy me off, with some measly bit of garden." He growled over his shoulder at her.

Ellen breathed in relief, even if he wasn't friendly, at least he was speaking to her at last. She moved a little nearer.

"I'm not trying to buy you off and I'm not trying to keep you out. That's the last thing I want." She whispered. "I'm giving you somewhere that none of my guests will be allowed to go. You can even fence it off if you want to." She could see the scarred side of his face. A muscle in his jaw was clenching and his hands were stiff at his sides.

"I don't want fences around my house. I don't want to be caged in. I'm not an animal. I bought this place to be alone not surrounded by hundreds of people." His voice was louder now.

She stepped back at his sudden ferocity. He sounded as though he hated her.

"Don't be angry with me Patrick. I've tried to see you about this, tried to talk to you, but you won't even look at me anymore." She felt her voice begin to crack. It was nothing to the sounds in her heart. It was shattered already.

Patrick turned his head a few degrees towards her.

"I never looked at you much anyway. I only saw you four times before in my whole life. I don't call that a close acquaintance. I don't see why I have to drop everything just because you call." His tone was spiteful, filled with hatred. He still had his back to her.

Suddenly she was angry. He was being so unfair. She walked slowly across the room and stood right behind him, wanting to touch him so desperately she had to ball her fists at her sides to stop herself.

"What have I done? You heard the plans. I would have thought you of all people would have been pleased." She swallowed back tears as she saw his body stiffen even more.

His chin came up.

"It all sounds a bit grim to me. All us cripples in one place. Maybe you expect us all to compare injuries. I don't understand why you're doing it. If it's some sort of fantasy, do-good thing, you can just forget it. You'll never make it pay." His voice was wound so tight she thought it was going to snap.

She kept her tone calm.

"I don't need to make it pay. Well, not from

those that need it most. You left before the end of the meeting, why don't you come up to the house and I'll show you everything in detail. I'm sure you will change your mind." She was pleading now.

"No! I don't want to see it and I don't want to see you. Can you just go?" He sounded as cold as stone.

She didn't move for a second. Her heart plummeted into her stomach and tears sprang to her eyes.

"Patrick, please don't say that. Please. I need to see you." She sobbed uncontrollably, unable to bear his words.

He dared a quick glance at her and saw the tears trembling, sparkling on her black lashes.

"Huh! Who the hell are you trying to kid? Your tears are only for yourself. They mean nothing to me. I hate you for what you are doing to me. Leave me alone. Get out of my house and just leave me alone." His voice suddenly crumpled and he moved away from the stove. He didn't even look back at her as he shoved his way past and through into another room. He slammed the door loudly behind him.

She stood quite still, completely stunned by his outburst and then she flew to the door.

The tears were nearly blinding her as she ran back to the Chateau. The bushes tore at her arms and face, but she didn't care. She wanted them to hurt. She wanted them to sting, burn, tear her flesh, anything to take away the pain in her heart.

By the time she was standing in front of the huge pile of scaffolding, she was shaking and near collapse. Her breath came in huge, desperate gasps. *He couldn't mean what he had said. It wasn't possible. How could he hate her so much?* She gulped in a huge lungful of air and then her mind blotted out all the pain as she saw the immense pile of metal and wood in front of her.

She sighed, trying not to think of how her arms were going to feel in the morning. It was probably just what she needed. Loading the truck was going to take her the rest of the evening and most of the night. So long as it took her mind off Patrick, she didn't care. She didn't think she could live if she ever thought of him again.

She tramped into the Chateau and pulled off her jacket and dress. She threw them back into her suitcase and dragged on her old jeans and T-shirt. Then she took a deep breath, went back outside to the colossal pile of metal, and lifted the first pole. It wasn't quite as heavy as she thought it might be and she hefted another up with it. She began to load them onto the truck.

Patrick stood by his bed breathing deeply.

He could barely think, let alone move. For nearly two months he had avoided her at all costs, not seeking her out or spying on her, not answering her calls or the door when she had knocked.

When he had seen her in the cellar with her fiancé, it had been terrible. He hadn't seen the blond man around the Chateau while Ellen was buying it and he had assumed that he was no longer in the picture. When he had arrogantly announced who he was as he sneered at Patrick and demanded directions to find Ellen, Patrick had wanted to kill the man, tear him apart with his bare hands for even existing. But that had been weeks ago, by now he had hoped he would be immune.

Less than thirty seconds in her company had seen him straight on that score.

She had looked so beautiful in her pretty yellow dress. Her brown eyes and hair so deep and lustrous, her lips so delicate, so soft, so kissable.

He wanted her with every fibre in his broken body. He wanted her so desperately he had to yell at her to leave or he would have grabbed her to him, taken her there and then. Her fragrance was in his nose, on his skin, in his house. It was impossible to escape.

He collapsed on his bed and pushed his hands through his hair. He wanted to tug it out by the roots, he wanted to tear his heart from his body and throw it for the crows to peck. He tried to control his breathing, but every lungful felt as though he had inhaled nails, he just wanted to scream with the pains that were stabbing deep into his chest.

Instead, he lay down on his bed and wept.

He didn't know how long it took him to cry himself dry, the pent up rage and frustration of the last two years seeping its way from his eyes to his pillow.

It felt as though an age had passed before he could see clearly again. His throat felt dry and raw, the scarred side of his face pricked with dried salty tears.

He sat up, hating himself for his display of weakness, then he stood and flung open the door of his room. He was almost afraid that she would still be there in his lounge, but the room was empty and still and the evening light was fading fast.

He drank a swig of cold tea from his mug still by the fire, shuddered with distaste even though it quenched his thirst, and then as he turned to see what he might have for dinner, he caught sight of the folder of papers on the table. He didn't want to be bothered to look at them, and for a few moments he considered throwing them into the fire, but eventually curiosity got the better of him and he opened the first page.

It was a deed of entitlement, written up in

French and then translated into English. He ran his finger along the main points, noting, with some surprise, that he still had rights of access to all parts of the estate, and then seeing that the parcel of land she was signing over to him was designated as a gift. He creased his eyebrows in concentration, then flipped over the page to see the ten foot she imagined would give him privacy. It was all marked in red pen on an official Plan Cadastral.

He stopped breathing as he looked at the red line surrounding the plot, not quite believing his own eyes. He took the papers to the window, checking in the last of the fading daylight. The line wasn't ten feet from his front door. It wasn't even a hundred feet from his door. The parcel of land was huge. It covered nearly a quarter of the whole estate, right down to the river on one side and to the road on the other.

He sat down hard on his wooden chair. There was no way she would give this amount of land away. Why would she? She didn't have to give him a thing. And whatever she gave him, it was no advantage to her. He could still march all over her property if he wanted.

This had to be a mistake. He looked at it all again. Perhaps someone had drawn the scale wrongly.

He pushed his chair back. This would need

sorting out right away. He didn't want to have to see her, but there was no way he could let this rest. He tucked the papers back in the folder and went to his bathroom to wash his face. He glanced up out of the window, surprised at how low the sun was in the sky. He couldn't think how so much time had passed while he had been in his room. He hoped she would still be about.

He grabbed up the folder and tucked it under his arm, then he closed his front door and began the long trudge up to the Chateau.

The soft clanking sound came to him when he was about half way along the path.

The workmen were obviously still there, loading up the huge pile of scaffolding that he had seen earlier in the day. For a moment he wondered why they were working so late, but then he breathed a sigh of relief. At least he wouldn't have to see her on her own. He didn't think he could trust himself to be near her alone.

It was only as he neared the Chateau that he realized that the men were working silently. It was strange. Normally they clattered and chattered all the time, friendly banter and jokes falling from their lips every second that they worked. The silence seemed so odd that he slowed his steps and peered through the bushes.

He could scarcely believe his own eyes.

She had changed her clothes. The pretty yellow dress was gone and she was back in her jeans and t-shirt, hoisting a couple of metal bars onto a shoulder that she had padded with a small square of thick cloth. She staggered, her tiny frame slightly unsteady, before she balanced them up and moved them to the side of the lorry. She tipped them up on end next to a line of about twenty more. Then she clambered into the back of the truck and began pulling each pipe up individually and laying it between the two stacks of scaffold boards already on the floor space.

He stood there watching her in amazement. When she had finished loading the twenty bars she jumped down from the lorry and began the whole process again. There were already about a hundred of the metal tubes on the lorry and the same in boards. His mouth dropped open as she went back to the still massive pile. *Was she really going to load the whole lot by herself?* Her hair was coming undone from the sparkly clip she always wore, floating about her pale face as she worked and he noticed how her slender arms trembled as she picked up the next lot of metal. This time she stopped by the side of the lorry and wiped her hand across her brow. He could see by the tension in her face that she was utterly exhausted.

He shook his head and pushed his way out of the bushes.

"What the heck do you think you are doing?" He grabbed the metal bar before it fell as she jumped in surprise. "Where are Sylvan and his men? They should be doing this." He flung the bar into the back of the truck as if it weighed no more than a feather.

She barely looked at him as she trudged back to the pile of metal.

"They finished taking this lot down this afternoon and didn't have the time to load it before they stopped for the day. This one must be done by the morning. As there's nobody else here, it's down to me to get it done. Now if you don't mind, unless you've anything important to say, can you please leave me to get on, otherwise I'm going to be here all night." She staggered under the weight of the three pipes on her shoulder and then tipped them upright ready for loading again.

"You're going to be here all night anyway. Look, don't be ridiculous Ellen. You can't do this by yourself." He stood in front of her as she retraced her steps for the next load.

She pushed past him, still not looking at him and lifted another three. This time the strain was even more visible.

"Well, I don't see anyone else around do

you?" She puffed past him, tipped the poles and stood by the lorry for a few seconds, catching her breath.

He looked up at the back of the lorry.

"Have you done all of this on your own? The boards too?"

She shrugged.

"Like I said, there's no one else here. I gave everyone the day off due to the meeting." She sighed wearily putting her hands on her hips as she glared up at him. "What do you want Patrick? Only a few hours ago you made it quite clear that you didn't want to see me again. Ever. What brings you running back to see me so soon after I was dismissed?" Her tone was harsh, but there was an underlying tremble that made him stare at her.

He swallowed before he spoke.

"I looked at the papers." He stopped as she turned her back on him, hoisted herself into the bed of the lorry and began pulling up pipes. The muscles in her arms looked like whipcord. She was a lot stronger than she first appeared, but that didn't mean a lot after the amount of lifting and carrying she had done. He felt beads of sweat spring to his brow. "Ellen, for goodness sake stop and listen. I said I looked over the papers."

She still didn't look at him. The pipes clanged loudly as she dropped them into the lorry.

"Good. Did you sign them? You can leave them inside on the table. The deeds will be sent to you direct from the Notaire. I believe it takes about three months to receive them, but the land will be yours from the moment you sign." She jumped back down from the truck again.

Patrick stepped up close to her, barring her way back to the pile of scaffold poles.

"I didn't sign them. There's an error with the scale on the plan." He held out the folder in front of him.

She looked at it for a few seconds, then stepped forwards and took the folder, careful not to make contact with his hand. Her eyes narrowed slightly.

"Really? I thought I checked them over quite carefully." She flipped open the pages, scanning them quickly, turning them to the little remaining light to make sure. "I can't see any problem with it. It's all drawn up legally. You're mistaken. I can't see that there's anything wrong with it at all." She closed the documents suddenly and handed the folder back to him.

He immediately flipped it back open onto the Plan Cadastral and pointed a long finger, tapping it on the red markings outlining the plot of land.

"Here! This red line around the amount of land. It's got to be wrong" He thrust the paper under her nose again.

She looked at it for less than a second and then brushed the papers aside.

"No, it's right. That's what I thought you would need." She pushed past him yet again, but this time he caught hold of her arm, stopping her in her tracks. She looked down at his hand. He let her go immediately.

"Why?" He breathed into the sudden silence, shocked at her generosity. "It's so much." He stared at her tired expression.

She shrugged almost dismissively.

"Not if you want your privacy and you've made it perfectly plain that you do. It's probably not quite enough, but I need the rest of the estate for my project, so I'm afraid you'll have to make do. Of course if you want to come and join in with anything going on here, you're very welcome, you do have access rights still. Just call me up first and I'll make sure I stay out of your way while you're over here." He heard the strain in her tone.

"Ellen, please listen to me. I didn't mean…I don't know what to say." He stood there uselessly.

"Just sign the papers Patrick, and then you can go. You'll never have to see me again and I'll never come to bother you, I promise." Her voice cracked this time and she slumped as she reached the never-ending metal heap. Her shoulders were shaking violently as she bent to gather more piping.

Patrick put the folder on the stone wall and walked over to her. He sounded almost awed.

"It's so much to give me." He touched her shoulder lightly, but she shook him off and spun away from him. "Ellen! I've got to say something." He raised his voice in desperation at her reaction.

More of her hair had come loose from her clip and it wafted about her face. She dragged it back and tugged it roughly into place, her fingers becoming entangled in the long vibrant stands. She gasped in pain and frustration and then suddenly she was tugging her hair hard, not caring as the soft strands pulled away from her scalp and drifted to the floor.

Tears began streaming down her face.

"Don't say anything to me Patrick! Don't speak to me ever again! Every time I hear your voice it just makes everything worse!" She shouted into the quiet evening, her anguish obvious.

She was sobbing uncontrollably as Patrick, unable to bear her distress, caught hold of her fingers. He wrapped his hand around hers and stopped her tearing anymore hair from her head. Then he pulled her hand down to her side. He didn't understand what she was saying. How could he make anything worse for her? She must be talking about the scaffolding.

"Stop it Ellen. Stop this now. You're exhausted and obviously not thinking straight. Leave all this to Sylvan and go to bed." His tone was gentle and he massaged her hand with his own. It was so small and soft, his hand felt huge and calloused around it.

"I can't!" She shouted again, nearly hysterical now, as she wrenched her hand out of his. "I have to get it done. He'll lose his next contract if I don't do it. I can't let that happen. I've only just got the town on my side. I can't ruin it all by letting down one of their biggest employers." She was swaying and, as she stepped sideways to move round him, she stumbled. Her foot caught on the uneven soil and she went sprawling towards the ground.

Patrick lurched to catch her, but he was off balance and his leg moved unevenly. He missed, his arms flailing hopelessly as she crashed into the pile of scaffolding.

She let out a pained cry as she rolled off the pile and slithered down onto the rough grass.

He regained his balance at last and shouted angrily.

"Ellen! Right, that's it! You just listen to me. You're going to bed right now before you kill yourself." He marched up to her and began to pull her up from the floor, but it was obvious her legs were not going to carry her. Her whole body drooped with exhaustion and before she could protest, he had scooped her up behind the knees, pulled her body into his chest and walked up the stone steps, carrying her into the Chateau.

"Where are you sleeping?" He asked as her head fell against his chest.

She breathed in his scent, unable to believe that she was at last in his arms. Even though it didn't mean anything to him, it was more than enough for her.

"Over there." She mumbled as she gave in and nodded to her right. He pushed through a makeshift curtain slung over a doorway, and into her bedroom. He looked aghast at the sleeping bag rolled out on the hard floor.

He stopped dead inside the doorway, staring at the bare floorboards, the loose material hung at the window.

"Is this where you've been sleeping for the last two months?" He didn't put her down as she nodded gently against his body. She could feel the hardness of his muscles clamped around her, and then knowing that he would soon be gone again, it became more than she could bear. She wriggled and tried to release herself from his grasp. His muscles contracted harder as he held her even tighter. "You can't stay here." He stated flatly.

"I'll be fine. I'm just so tired. Put me

down." Her voice was almost a whisper.

"Not a chance, you need a proper bed." He spoke with finality, turned swiftly out of the room and back out of the Chateau.

"What are you doing? Patrick, put me down." She protested, her voice weak. He ignored her pleas and marched back along the forest path as she struggled feebly in his arms.

It was hopeless. She was too exhausted to break his iron grasp. She stopped fighting him and relaxed at last.

She was so light in his arms that she barely registered as there. Her head fell back after less than a minute of his steady pace and he looked down at her now sleeping form, noticing for the first time how her cheekbones were so prominent in her perfect face and how he could feel her ribs through her t-shirt.

He shouldered his way through the front door, glad that he never bothered locking it and then straight on into his bedroom. He pulled back the covers with one hand and laid her down gently. She didn't stir at all. He pulled her boots from her feet and she curled in sideways. She looked tiny in his bed. He stared at her sleeping figure for a few seconds, wishing that she were there under very different circumstances, then he pulled his quilt over her, closed the door quietly and trudged out of his house and back up to the Chateau.

Chapter Six

Ellen snuggled into the plump pillow. It was so soft, so comfortable and it smelt so delicious. She breathed in deeply, taking in the wonderful smell and was about to snuggle into it again when she realized what she was doing. She opened her eyes in shock.

She launched herself forwards and then brought her hands to her head as a multitude of stars exploded in her brain. She had sat up too fast.

She closed her eyes again and listened to her pounding heart. She knew immediately where she was. She could smell him all around her. She felt down her body, not sure if she was relieved that she was alone and still fully clothed. She pushed her hair away from her face, opened her eyes again and cast them across the bed. The stars were still all around her and she realized that they weren't in her head, but coming from her clip that was lying on the dressing table. She reached out, picked it up, twisted her hair into a knot, and clipped it. Then she looked around the small but beautiful bedroom.

The bed was huge, taking up most of the available space. What looked like a handmade quilt was turned over at the bottom of the bed. The surface of the dressing table was clean and shining. There was a small bottle of scent at one side. The shape of the bottle was unusual. It was engraved with wild swirling patterns. She looked a little closer. Penhaligons perhaps? She wasn't sure, the sun was shining too brightly onto it. She sat back for a moment trying to think.

What in God's name was she doing here? The last thing she could remember was Patrick moaning about the parcel of land that she was giving him. She stared out of the window, trying to remember anything else and then she realized that the sun was shining in from the wrong side of the house. It wasn't evening. It was morning. She had been there all night!

She groaned as it all came flooding back to her. And then she remembered the scaffolding.

She gasped in dismay and swung her legs out of the huge bed. She was about to stand up when there was a gentle knock on the door. Patrick came in holding two mugs of tea in his hands.

"I thought I heard you stir. I didn't put any sugar in it. Sorry, I don't take it myself and there's none in the house." He sat on the bed beside her.

She looked over at him and took the proffered mug.

"Thanks. It's fine. I don't take sugar either." She sipped the steaming liquid gratefully. They were silent for a few seconds then she stood up. "Thanks for letting me get a decent night's sleep. I obviously needed it…I have to go. I must apologise to Sylvan about the scaffolding. I'll just have to pay his extra fees." She put the mug on the dressing table.

"Sylvan left hours ago. It's nearly twelve." Patrick sipped more of his tea.

"Oh no! I bet he was as mad as hell. Why did you let me sleep so long?" She slumped back onto the bed.

The unscarred corner of Patrick's mouth twitched in a small smile.

"Actually he was quite happy. I loaded most of the rest of the scaffolding last night after I'd got you tucked up in here. You'd never have managed it. I'm way tougher than you and it took me until nearly four this morning." He looked down at her obviously pleased with himself.

Her mouth fell open.

"You loaded the truck for me? Why?" She was completely taken aback. She didn't think he'd wanted to have anything to do with her or her project.

He shrugged.

"Because you were going to kill yourself doing it. You were completely out of it when I brought you back here last night Ellen." He paused for a moment, looking at her carefully. "Why don't you have a real bed up there? You obviously haven't slept properly for months, it's no wonder you're so exhausted." He was staring at her, his blue eyes deeply concerned.

She wrapped her hands back around the mug, just to give herself something to do. He was so close, it was difficult not to reach out and touch him. She wanted to grab hold of him and pull him close, she wanted to run her fingers through his long, dark hair, she wanted to feel his body on hers. Instead, she held onto the mug, gripping it as though her life depended on it.

"I just didn't get round to it yet. I have to keep moving my room about, depending on where I'm working in the Chateau. It just seemed easier to throw down a sleeping bag. It's fine. I used to go camping all the time when I was younger." She tried not to look at the horribly comfortable bed on which she was sitting.

He snorted dismissively.

"Not for months at a time though. Even the army doesn't expect you to do that. It's too knackering."

She lifted her shoulders.

"It's not as though I had much choice. The hotel didn't want me as their guest after they saw what I was doing and I couldn't be far away. I'm managing this project by myself and I have to be on site all the time. If I'm not there, absolutely nothing gets done. The men hate taking orders from a woman and what with their working times! I had no idea that the French work such short hours. Half the time I feel as though they only work three days a week. Honestly Patrick, it's been a nightmare and I haven't even started on the inside." Talking about the Chateau made her feel safe enough to put her mug down again. She reached for her boots.

Patrick lowered his gaze guiltily.

"I am so sorry Ellen. I've been an absolute idiot. You must hate me for making things even more difficult for you." He picked up the empty mugs and walked back out of the room, unable to meet her eyes.

She left her boots beside the bed and followed him closely, pleased that they now seemed to be able to hold some sort of conversation.

"Forget it. You weren't the only one to object to the proposal. It was probably as much my fault as anyone's. I should have been more open about it, but I wanted to keep it to myself until I was sure I could do it."

He turned to look at her for a moment.

"You should have told me, Ellen."

She laughed half-heartedly, thinking of the times he had ignored her calls.

"And just how would I have done that? You have been avoiding me like the plague since I first viewed the place. I've only seen you once in nearly three months and then you completely blanked me."

He stammered, more embarrassed than he cared to admit.

"I…I was busy. I had a lot to do."

"Like what Patrick?" She scoffed.

He fiddled with some wood by the stove and didn't meet her gaze. And then suddenly he gave a great sigh.

"Like avoiding you, for one. Actually avoiding you, full stop." He confessed at last, busying himself with the stove again, wishing she wasn't so close to him.

"Why? Why do you want to avoid me? What have I done to you?" She spoke so quietly he looked over to her.

And then he gave up trying to hide it. He couldn't conceal his feelings any longer. He didn't know whether she would understand his true meaning, but he had to tell her something. He would just have to take the pain of rejection.

"You haven't done anything." His voice was agonized. "It's just me. I can't be near you. Last night, knowing you were lying in my bed, was nearly killing me. It's just as well I spent most of the night loading that lorry." He shook his head. "I can't have you close to me Ellen, it's too painful." He swallowed noisily and the pulse in his throat started to pound.

Ellen creased her brow in confusion.

"I don't understand Patrick. How do I hurt you? I wouldn't hurt you ever." She looked down at the floor, unable to bear looking into his eyes.

He risked putting his hand under her chin and lifting it gently. She had to understand how he felt. He couldn't disguise it any longer. Her eyes met his.

"Don't you see Ellen? Can't you see how much these scars hurt me? They have ruined my life. Everything that I'd known before ended in less than a second. Everything. To have someone as beautiful as you see what I've become just makes it all so much worse." He was whispering now and his whole body was very still.

She was confused for a few seconds and then she saw the smouldering in his eyes. It was as though a curtain had been swished away. Her heart broke and she wanted to cry for him.

"But they're only scars Patrick. They will fade. I don't even notice them." Her voice was cracking, her lips trembling. She sounded as desolate as he felt.

He glared down at her. *Was she mocking him?* A tidal wave of fury welled up in him.

"Fade! How the hell does having no leg fade? How do you get rid of burns like these?" His head came up and he was shouting now. "Every single morning I get up, look in the mirror and I pray, I pray so hard, that they'll be gone, that it was all some sort of freaky nightmare, but there's always this grotesque character staring back at me. Someone I don't recognize, someone I don't even know. It feels as though the real me doesn't exist anymore. How the hell can you not notice scars like these? You're just pretending they're not there Ellen! They'll never go and I can't ignore them. Oh! I don't care anymore. I just don't care! Look at them, see for yourself how repulsive I am!" He was tugging his shirt from his waistband. He pulled at the buttons savagely and ripped the fabric from his shoulders. He stood naked to the waist, not looking at her, breathing hard.

She looked up at his glorious body. His right shoulder and side were perfect. Tanned and firm and defined, ripples of hard muscle spreading from his neck, across his shoulder, over his chest and down onto his flat stomach.

His left side was in tatters. The scars that covered this side of his face just touched the corner of his mouth, then crept down over his neck. There were deep red hollows across his left shoulder and chunks of muscle missing from his arm and then a cruel spider's web of lumpy marks trailing over his wide chest, fading slightly as they reached his waistline. She stepped closer to him and reached her hand up to touch his mutilated skin.

He moved fast and grabbed it before she could lay a finger on him.

"Don't!" He snarled at her and her eyes flicked up to his face. She moved in closer, unafraid of him now, his hand still tightly over hers.

And then before he was able to stop her she leaned in, laid her satin cheek gently on his bare chest and listened to his thundering heart.

"I don't see the scars Patrick." She whispered, her lips just touching his fevered skin. "I see only you. I want only you." Her breath was moist and warm on his flesh.

He dropped her hand as if he'd been electrocuted and moved away quickly. His control was at breaking point.

"Don't lie to me Ellen. I know the truth, I'm repulsive. You can't want me, so don't try and make me think you do. It hurts too much. My own wife left me as soon as she saw me like this, she was so appalled, so don't tell me you see anything different." His words were full of bitterness. He bent to pick up his shirt, but Ellen was there first. She grabbed it from the floor, flung it behind her and stood defiantly in front of him.

And then she tugged at the bottom of her t-shirt and lifted it over her head. She threw it to land on top of his shirt.

He gasped and then groaned deeply as she

put her hands behind her back and unclasped her bra.

He couldn't take his eyes off her as the wisp of delicate material fell from her shoulders.

Her breasts were high and firm, her nipples rosy and tight against her milk white skin.

She stretched forwards, caught hold of his hand and brought it to her lips. Her kisses felt as soft as feathers against his skin. Then she placed his hand gently over her breast.

The feel of her soft, tender flesh within his palm finished him. He could hold back no longer. He pulled in a deep, ragged breath as he massaged her breast, letting his thumb stroke her tightening nipple.

"Why are you doing this to me? It's hard enough for me to just be with you, without you doing this as well." He gasped out the words.

She smiled gently and looked down at his hand. She groaned as her nipple peaked against his skin. Then spoke breathlessly.

"Because now I know what this is all about. At last. I want you Patrick. I wanted you from the moment you first spoke to me. It was no lie, and I know you want me too."

She began to undo her jeans and he just stood there staring helplessly at her as they slithered to the floor. Then she stepped out of them and moved even closer to him. She reached out and began to unfasten his belt. She pushed his trousers past the cup on his leg, onto the floor, then she took his hand in hers and led him silently back to his bedroom.

They lay spent and gasping, the roar of his agonized release still ringing in her ears as the sheets tangled around them. Their perspiration was drying on their naked bodies. He was still on top of her, still deep inside her, and they were both still breathing hard.

Patrick pressed his forehead into her shoulder, barely able to comprehend what had just happened. It had been over in minutes, both too frantic with pent up desire to think about making it last. But it had been the most intense few minutes of his entire life. Her hair had come out of the clip again and he could feel it covering his face. He could hear the rapid thumping of her heart. He bent a little further and caught her nipple between his lips. It tightened instantly. He swirled his tongue over the hard bud and listened to Ellen moan in pleasure.

He had never felt emotions like this in his whole life. He lay there, bathed in a glow of complete satisfaction, in a wave of glory so intense he wanted to shout for joy. He felt her move slightly under his weight and he lifted his head to look at her beautiful face.

Her fabulous eyes were closed, her long lashes almost touching her flushed cheeks, and a small, satisfied smile was playing about the corners of her perfect lips. She looked as content as he felt.

"Ellen?" He whispered, checking. "Are you okay?"

The smile became wider. She nodded and stretched slightly and then grimaced.

"Sorry." She opened her eyes. "Can you just move your leg?" He lifted his hip slightly and she gasped as the silicone cup pulled away from her skin.

He looked down in horror as he saw where the moulding of his prosthetic limb had grazed her inner thigh.

"God damn this thing!" He spoke bitterly. "I'm sorry. I didn't think. I've not done anything like this since before it happened." He struggled to get up, but she held onto his shoulders, forcing him to be still.

"No, stay here. Now that I have you, I don't want you to move. We'll just have to remember to take it off next time." She let her fingers trail lazily through his hair.

He lay back down again and sighed deeply.

"So there is going to be a next time then?" He could hardly bear to ask.

She pulled in an indignant breath and glared

at him.

"I should bloody well hope so! After all the misunderstanding and effort it's taken to get you, I should hope there will be quite a few next times." She smiled into his hair.

"Why didn't you just tell me? I was driving myself mad avoiding you. I thought you would be repulsed by me." He lifted his head and looked into her eyes.

Her hair tumbled about her shoulders as she shook her head.

"Why? I never once gave you any reason to make you think I might find you unattractive. I fell in love with you before I even saw you, the night you rescued me. I sat up the whole night while my fiancé puked his guts up, just wanting to smell you again. I sat with your coat around me the whole night long."

He grunted.

"So that's why it was covered with your scent. I thought you might have sprayed it to get rid of the smell of the wood smoke. I nearly came and asked for it back. I followed you after I'd sent you in the right direction. I was telling myself it was to make sure you didn't go the wrong way down the road, but it wasn't that really. I just wanted to keep looking at you." He smiled sheepishly up at her.

She laughed.

"That's nothing. I thought I was going to go mad with you being so close to me when you were showing me the Chateau. And when we nearly kissed, you suddenly hesitated. I was so angry with Anton. If he hadn't kicked that stone at the crucial moment everything might have been different. I thought afterwards, when you nearly fell and seemed so furious, that I was wrong about the way you were feeling, that you didn't like me at all."

He pulled her down to him again and pressed his lips gently to hers, savouring the taste of her before he replied.

"No, I was trying very hard not to take you on that filthy floor. I never wanted anything so much in my whole life. It was taking every bit of my self-control just to keep my hands off you. I had to stand in a cold shower for over an hour when I got back here. When you came here yesterday, I thought I was going to attack you. I had to get you away from me. I thought I was losing it completely. The last few months have been sheer hell."

She breathed out slowly.

"And I thought I was making my feelings clear. I thought you would see what I was feeling. I felt so different, so new and I was so glad to be away from Justin."

Patrick suddenly froze beside her, remembering her fiancé's visit. His tone was hard.

"But you still have Justin. I showed him up here not long after you bought the place if you remember." He pushed himself out of her arms. "Hang on. Oh! I get it now. I know what's really going on here!"

She grabbed him back, clutching his shoulders hard as she spoke desperately, knowing exactly what was going through his mind.

"I broke it off with him after I first met you, and then I had to tell him again the next morning as soon as he was sober enough to listen to me. I can't believe I put up with him for so long. It took me over three years to realize what a self-centered idiot he is. I tried to tell you when you came up to the Chateau the day you directed him, but you wouldn't listen. You walked off. Hey! What's the matter?" She asked as he wrenched himself away from her. She sat up and pulled the duvet around her.

Patrick flopped back onto his side of the bed. He wiped his hand across his face, thinking hard.

"You broke it off that first night? Really? I don't believe you. You can't possibly have thought like that about me after one chance meeting. You hadn't even seen me. You can't fall in love with a smell." He closed his eyes again, breathing hard as he tried to overpower his temper that was threatening to rage out of control.

She spoke gently, moving closer to him again.

"I didn't need to see you to know I was in love with you. If Anton hadn't been there that day when you showed me the Chateau, you wouldn't have stood a chance. And yesterday, well, if it hadn't been such a long, stressful day and if I hadn't had to get that blasted lorry loaded, I might have tried a bit harder." She ran her fingertips along the scars on his face.

He snatched at her hand, pulling it away from his tattered skin. He opened his eyes, suddenly even more furious.

He growled out his words.

"Stop it Ellen. You're just saying these things. I know the truth! This is all just some elaborate plan to get me out of your hair. Did you and your fiancé cook this scenario up when he came to visit you? Is this what you argued over? Did he convince you that having sex with me would swing my vote?" He sat up quickly and swung his legs over the side of the bed. He took a few deep breaths and tried to calm his racing, breaking heart. "Look it's okay. I get it now. You just used me, but don't worry, I'm not holding you to anything. This was just a one off, okay. You don't have to lie to me about your fiancé anymore." He began dragging a pair of jeans over his legs.

Ellen sat stunned for a second, not knowing whether to be more angry than upset. Then she saw the agonized look on his face. She could almost feel his pain.

Her voice cracked.

"Patrick! Don't say that. I'm not using you and I'm not trying to trick you or lie to you either. Why do you think I wouldn't tell you the truth?" She was scrabbling to get out of the bed after him.

He threw her clothes onto the bed and pulled on his shirt. He couldn't bear to look at her delicious body again. The thought of giving her up now nearly killed him on the spot, but he took in a ragged breath and then breathed it out slowly.

"Come on, get dressed. This meant nothing. I'll sign those papers and let you get back on with your life. You can go back to him now. I'll stay out of your way." His tone was resigned as he stood up and moved towards the door.

She dropped the duvet and swung her legs over the side of the bed. His dismissive, disinterested tone made her see red.

"What the hell are you talking about? I'm not going back to him! I didn't want to see him that day he showed up here, and I don't want to ever again. He was threatening me. He just wanted more money. If you had arrived only a few moments earlier you would know that I'm not lying." She was shaking in distress, desperate to convince him. "I'm telling the truth Patrick. And why would I need to seduce you now anyway? I already have the permits. I love you. Do you need more proof?"

He was suddenly very still again, watching her carefully. There was something frantic in her tone. And then she came up to him and wrapped her arms around his neck. The fabric of the shirt he had dragged over his shoulders, rubbed against her naked breasts. Her nipples peaked against him.

He was staring at her incredulously. It just couldn't be true. She couldn't love him. It wasn't possible that someone so beautiful could love someone so ruined.

But she was still there, standing defiantly in front of him. Close, warm, soft, fragrant and fabulous and still completely naked.

She stepped in even nearer, pressing her slender body against him, moulding herself to him.

"Do you need me to prove it to you? Patrick?" She asked again, her hands were in his hair now, her fingers running gently over his scalp, her lips hot and moist on his neck.

He pulled himself away and tipped her chin back searching deep into her dark eyes, expecting mockery, expecting lies. He saw only the truth and the deepest desire pooled there. His whole being calmed, but his blood began to race again. He felt his passion throb and harden. He lifted his hand to her face, cupping it gently and tipping her chin further. He felt her sweet breath flood over him.

"Do I need you to prove that you love me?" He asked as his gaze drowned in hers. "Oh God yes!" He whispered, crushing her lips with his own as he began tearing off his shirt.

They didn't surface until the evening. They had made love frantically again, desperate for each other, then dozed for half the afternoon, and then they joined together yet again. Slowly, sensuously this time. Hours passed, touching, tasting, exploring.

As the light began to fade through the trees outside the window, a soft chirping sound roused them. Ellen leaned over the side of the bed and began to search through their discarded heap of clothes, for her mobile phone.

"Don't answer it" Patrick murmured. He rolled over and dragged her back to his side.

She snuggled into his broad chest.

"What time is it?" She asked lazily.

"About seven I think. Maybe later. Why? Do you have anything you're meant to be at?" He curled a strand of her hair round his finger and tugged gently, bringing her face level with his. She put her lips on his, flicking her tongue over his teeth, then moved back again.

"No, it's just that David normally rings about now, if he's not on duty."

Patrick raised his eyebrows in surprise.

"On duty? Doing what? I thought you said he's a double amputee." He propped himself up on his elbow, suddenly interested.

She looked up at him, rolling her eyes as she traced the lines of his scars with her fingertip. He shuddered slightly, but didn't stop her. Ellen dropped her finger.

"I said he'd lost his legs and most of his face, not his brain. He works in army intelligence now. Most of his mates are there too. They all took on office jobs after being wounded in active service. I'm surprised that you didn't do something similar." The phone had stopped ringing. "Oh well, I'll just have to speak to him some other time."

Patrick relaxed back in the bed, but then his stomach gave a huge growl.

Ellen laughed.

"All the exercise made you hungry?"

"Starving. We missed breakfast and lunch. Guy my size needs feeding regularly. Come on let's see what I've got hanging around." He leaned over the side of the bed and grabbed his prosthetic leg from the floor. He winced as he tried to force the cradle onto his severed limb. "Damn. I've damaged it. It fell when I pulled it off."

She watched over his shoulder as he tugged it back into shape. It creaked ominously.

"Well, you were in rather a hurry to get rid of it." She giggled and pulled his shirt over her head. It dropped to past her thighs. His stomach gave another huge rumble and he jammed the leg onto the stump of his thigh.

He stood up at last.

"I think there's some cassoulet left from yesterday. Fancy that?" He asked her. "It's home made." He lugged on some clothes.

"Hmm, lovely. I don't cook a lot, not that I could do much cooking at the Chateau anyway. I've only just had the electricity put on in the kitchen. I've been living off bread and cheese and cheap Champagne for the last eight weeks."

Patrick laughed as he bustled about the kitchen.

"Doesn't sound too bad to me."

Half an hour later they were tucking into deliciously tender pork loins covered with garlic, onions and haricot beans. He opened a bottle of red wine and poured it into beautifully fine wine glasses. They talked quietly as they ate.

"So what are you really thinking of doing with the place. As you said, I left the meeting early and didn't hear the full plans." He put a last morsel into his mouth and chewed slowly.

She looked up suddenly. She hadn't thought about her project all day. She thought about why, and smiled.

"You stayed to hear that it's going to be a hotel for people with disabilities. The forces especially. I want somewhere fabulous that you can go. To relax with the family and not even think about being stared at or if the right equipment might be available. I want people to know they will be completely looked after, but also have the independence they crave. I want the kids to have a great time with mum and dad, not even considering what other people might think of their parents."

Patrick laid his fork on his empty plate.

"Huh! Sounds great if it's families but if it's just us blokes then I still think it sounds a bit grim. It'll be like something out of a horror movie. Like I said before, who'd want to see all us cripples shoved in one place all together." He took another sip of wine.

Ellen couldn't help it. She laughed out loud, then stifled her giggles behind her hand.

"Cripple! For Goodness Sake! After what we just did all afternoon! Give yourself a little credit Patrick. You must be the least crippled bloke I know." Her eyes shone in merriment.

He smiled widely back at her, suddenly feeling a little stupid. He puffed out his chest as her words stroked his undernourished ego.

"Okay, I'll give you that one, but there are a lot of blokes worse off than me. Your David for one. Can't be much fun for him."

Ellen raised her eyebrows.

"Don't you ever let him hear you say anything like that Patrick or he'll show you just how crippled he isn't. And most of his mates are the same. They're all as tough as old boots and even if they're not, they'll never show it. It's not going to be grim Patrick. All those chaps and the women too, they'll be able to bring their families to somewhere they'll all enjoy, without all the fuss of ridiculous theme parks, where dad can't go on anything and everyone is staring or they are all worrying about who has the key to the disabled loo. They'll all love the woods and the river. I'm putting in a luxury spa and a huge pool and sauna in the basement. The restaurant is going to be fantastic, with a blazing fire and a hog roast or barbeques outside in the summer. There's going to be a cinema in the attic and a piano bar in the great hall. We're going to have black tie balls and parties for the kids." She was animated and the red wine glistened on her lips.

He was staring at her in awe.

"Okay, I agree it sounds great. When you put it like that I'd even book to come myself, but it's going to cost a bomb. With all that lot going on, and the condition of your clients, you're going to need plenty of staff and a lot of specialist equipment. You're only going to have maybe twenty rooms available to rent out. No bank is going to listen to it as a business proposition and us army guys don't have the cash for that kind of holiday anyway. Most of us are lucky if we can afford a weekend at Butlins. I know we get compensation for our injuries, but that's all eaten up just trying to live, that's if you get any at all. I was blown up over two years ago and I've still only had a small interim payment. They are still haggling over how much they think my leg was worth. I think you're wasting your time even thinking about it."

She caught hold of his hand and squeezed it gently.

"Oh Patrick, do you think I haven't thought about the funding. I've got some ideas to make up any shortfall. Let me worry about the money. Just at this moment, I'm rather more worried about you letting me stay here again tonight. I don't think I can face that sleeping bag after a night and day in your wonderful bed."

He leaned forwards and brushed a stray strand of hair from across her forehead. His fingers were warm and gentle. He massaged her cheek with his thumb, gazing deeply into her dark eyes.

His voice was suddenly husky with

emotion.

"Do you think I'd be so stupid as to let you go ever again? I've never met anyone like you before, and I've never felt like this before either Ellen. I only ever want to feel like this from now on. For the whole of the rest of my life." His hand slipped inside the collar of the shirt she had pulled on and he caressed her across her shoulder. Her skin was smooth and incredibly soft. "I love you." He whispered.

She leaned towards him, her eyes full of desire again.

"Does that mean I can stay?" She asked quietly as she pushed the plates to one side.

He stood up quickly, shoving his chair back to the wall as he dragged the table out from between them. He took a step forwards, placed his hands on her shoulders and pulled her up into his arms. He held her tight against him as he bent his head to hers.

"Forever." He whispered back. Then his mouth covered hers, his tongue tasting deeply as all thoughts of any more conversation disappeared in a haze of passion.

Chapter Seven

"What time does your brother get here?" Patrick was leafing through some colour charts, comparing them with the splodges of brownish goo smeared onto a board in front of him.

Ellen came and stood close beside him, her arm brushing his. She could feel the warmth of his skin through his linen shirt. She tried to concentrate on the coloured goo.

"Not until the morning. They're taking the overnight ferry. I can't wait for you to meet him and his mates. You lot are going to get on like a house on fire. It's a pity they are only here for a week, you'll barely have time to get to know each other." She sighed miserably.

Patrick frowned down at her.

"Well, why doesn't he stay longer? I thought he was meant to be doing this hotel thing with you. Does he have to go so soon?" He made himself sound disappointed. He would only have to share her for a week. He wanted to keep her to himself, but he also wanted her to be happy.

Ellen leaned forwards to peer at the splodge covered board with Patrick.

"He only has one week of leave. He's back on duty next Monday." Ellen linked Patrick's arm and considered the colours with him. She tapped her finger under a mellow beige.

Patrick smiled knowingly.

"That's the one Jean-Paul and I thought you would choose. It tones really well with the original stone in the house. We're going to keep as much of it exposed as possible. He'll be pleased at your choice." They were looking at the colour samples of possible new plaster.

Since they had been together, he had thrown himself into helping her with the Chateau. He was surprised at how much he was enjoying it. He looked down at her and put the colour chart on the table.

"Come here." He grabbed her round the waist, unable and unwilling to resist her. "I love you woman." He kissed her on the top of her head and then moved to kiss her lips.

She lifted her chin and gave them to him willingly groaning as his tongue flicked tantalizingly across her lips and into her mouth. She pulled back, not wanting him to get carried away. It was so easy to let him. It was so easy for her to give herself to him. But there were builders about today. He didn't let her go but nuzzled in at her neck instead. She sighed deeply.

"Yes, I know you love me. You told me so not half an hour ago." She snuggled against him, pressing her head into his hard chest. "I haven't told David about us yet. He's expecting me to sleep

166

here."

It was early September. Three months had passed since she and Patrick had first made love. They had spent every night together since. Three deliciously perfect months.

Patrick frowned down at her. He might be able to grudgingly share daytimes, but he certainly wasn't giving her up at night too.

"Well, he can expect all he likes. We haven't fixed up a room for the two of us here yet, and I'm not sure I even want one." He looked down at her, knowing how much she loved his tiny cottage, and waited until she nodded her head in agreement. "And you're not staying here without me. Not with a bunch of red blooded males on the loose." She gave him a playful slap on his arm. He smiled widely now, knowing he had nothing to fear. "So we're sleeping at mine. I'm not willing to give you up entirely, not even for a day, let alone a whole week, not even for a devoted brother. He'll get used to it. You're staying with me and that's that." He sighed deeply as he let her wriggle from his arms at last. "Claude is waiting for you in the hall. He wants you to test out the lift. He thinks it's running a bit slow." Patrick was referring to the local electrician.

Ellen opened her eyes wide.

"Slow! That's just not an option. I know how you army guys are. I'd better go and take a look." She turned towards the great hall, but then stopped as she heard a car pull up on the stones outside. "Who's that? It's not the bed people. Are we expecting anyone else today?" She was peering out of the window at a small red car that had pulled up on the forecourt.

He followed her gaze, his eyes narrowing as the car drew to a halt.

"Not that I kn…" His voice faded as a flame haired woman stepped out of the car. "Oh My God! What on earth is she doing here?" He asked in surprise as he started for the door immediately.

"Who is it?" Ellen was trying to look past his shoulder but he kept pushing her back.

Patrick's tone was icy. He pressed her backwards.

"It's no one. Look, why don't you go and sort out the electricity with Claude and then go and find Jean-Paul to confirm the plaster. I'll see to this and catch up with you later." He barred her way.

Ellen was not about to be put off.

"Patrick. Who is it? She's so beautiful." She was leaning round him now, staring through the window at the side of the door. The woman was stretching as she climbed from the car, her flame red hair glinting in the sunshine, her never ending legs looking bronzed and fabulous in the tiniest of tight skirts.

Patrick pushed Ellen back roughly. She staggered against the doorframe as he glared at her.

"Don't come out. I'll get rid of her right now." His voice came out like grit on stone as he moved quickly towards the huge front doors.

Ellen jumped forwards.

"Patrick! What's going on? Who is she?" Ellen demanded, grabbing his arm.

He spun back round and stared at her desperately. He took a massive breath.

"I'm so sorry Ellen. I didn't even know she knew that I lived here. I certainly never told her. Ellen…God! I am so sorry but that's Diane…My wife." His voice was as hopeless as his look.

Ellen let go of his arm as if she had been burned by him, and tried to sound neutral but her voice quivered slightly.

"Oh! Your wife? I thought you said she'd left you?" Her whole stomach had fallen to her knees. She stared out of the window again, mesmerized by the vision of beauty before her.

He was still trying to block her view.

"She did leave me. Three days after she first saw me in the hospital after I was blown up. She sent me a letter telling me that she couldn't see me again, that all my stuff was being sent to my parents. That was nearly three years ago. I haven't seen or heard from her since. Look, go and sort the electrics. I'll get rid of her." He strode through the doors, giving Ellen no time to argue.

She stared after him, too stunned to move.

The woman was turning, her hair swirling about her shoulders in the autumn breeze. She saw Patrick and gave a radiant smile as he walked down the stone steps to her. Ellen saw Patrick stiffen as the woman swept towards him, hips swinging in a slow, tantalizing rhythm. She wrapped her arms around his neck, then stood on her tiptoes and kissed him full on the lips.

Ellen gasped in shock. Patrick just stood there almost transfixed then he stepped backwards. Ellen heard him speak first.

"How did you find me Diane?" His tone was cool, disinterested.

The woman gave a low laugh.

"Oh Pat. I am still your wife. If you thought I couldn't find out where you lived, you really have lost the plot. I never imagined the place to be this grand though. It's fantastic. I can't believe you didn't tell me about it. I could do so much with it." Her voice dripped like smooth honey from her perfectly rouged lips.

Patrick was standing stiffly. He wiped the back of his hand over his mouth before he spoke.

"This isn't my place. I live over there through the forest. I was here seeing a friend. Why are you here anyway Diane?" He was removing her arms from where she had wound them around his neck, his voice was tense. She linked his arm with hers.

"Oh, so this belongs to a friend." She looked back up at the Chateau. Ellen whipped away from the window as the woman's voice dripped on. "You must introduce us sometime. As to your other question, well, I just came for a little visit. We haven't seen each other in so long. Time flies and all that, but there are some things we have to discuss. I must say you're looking good Pat. Better than when you left me." She laughed lightly.

A muscle flexed in his jaw. He barely opened his mouth as he spoke.

"If you remember, it was you that left me. Lying flat on my back in a hospital bed, three days after I'd been blown up..." He paused, breathing hard at the memory. "Look, let's get out of here. If you want to discuss anything, we can do it back at my place." He took hold of the woman's elbow, turned her away from the Chateau and guided her into the forest without so much as a backwards glance.

Ellen stood almost paralysed. She was sure her heart had stopped beating and then it was suddenly hammering in her chest. Time stood still as she stared out of the window at the driveway. If the little red car hadn't been sitting on the gravel she would have thought that the last few minutes had been part of a nasty dream.

There was a small cough behind her. She turned and saw a round, dark haired man, standing patiently holding up a length of electric cable. Ellen had no idea of how long he had been standing there. It could have been a minute or an hour or a day. She stared dumbly at him.

The man's voice came at her as though he were in a very long tunnel. It seemed as though his mouth opened and words came out and then sometime in the future she heard the sounds.

"Are you able to see the elevator now? Monsieur Patrick said you would test it. I can make some alterations if necessary." His words echoed around numbly in her head and then suddenly reached through the fog to her semi-paralysed brain.

"Yes...Yes of course Claude. I'm sorry. I was a little preoccupied. Tell me what you want me to see." She followed him blindly, as he led the way back into the great hall.

The rest of the day passed in a flurry of work. She approved the plaster with Jean-Paul and had Claude checking all the electrics again. She began planning colours of paint and flicked through catalogues of curtain material. She went over the number of shutters with the carpenter and took delivery of a few pieces of furniture. She telephoned the specialist bed company to make sure they were delivering her special order that afternoon, and then sat and made several appointments to see pool manufacturers and home cinema experts. At seven sharp the workmen all left.

The red car didn't.

It was still on the driveway at eight.

It was still on the driveway at nine.

Patrick didn't return from his cottage.

Ellen sat alone reviewing the next days' work in the Chateau. Silence surrounded her. At nine-thirty her stomach rumbled. She stood up slowly, her legs feeling like lead, and walked through to the kitchen. Her footsteps echoed loudly on the stone floor. She put the kettle on for a cup of tea. The sound of the kettle boiling drowned out the sound of deafening silence around her. She peered in the fridge to see what she might cook, but although it was completely full, in expectation of hungry guests, there was nothing that looked as though it would take the bitter taste from her mouth. She closed the fridge door and turned to the huge kitchen table. There was half a baguette left on a board. She picked it up and nibbled a corner of the bread. It tasted stale and dry. She dropped it back onto the board. She wasn't hungry.

She forgot her hot tea, grabbed a bottle of

wine from the rack and a glass from the cupboard. She walked out of the kitchen and began to climb the wide staircase. She didn't know what to do. She wanted to see Patrick. She wanted to hear him telling her that he loved her and that there was nothing for her to worry about. She looked back down the stairs, out to the drive. The little car was still there, gloating at her, mocking her. She sat on a small chair at the head of the stairs and waited. She opened the bottle of wine and had drunk more than half of it before she decided that he wasn't coming back.

He was spending the night at his home with his wife.

She put the bottle on the floor by the chair. She couldn't be bothered to take it back down to the kitchen.

She didn't stay on the first floor. All the rooms there had been prepared for her imminent guests and although they weren't finished or in any way luxurious yet, she didn't want to spoil what she had achieved. She ran up the next two flights of stairs and ducked into one of the tiny attic rooms. There were boxes piled on the floor. She tugged on the cardboard flap of one and pulled out her old sleeping bag. She threw it onto the bare floorboards, watching the dust swirl about her ankles in the fading light, and climbed in fully dressed.

She lay staring up at the high ceiling. A

chill seeped through the thin sleeping bag as she lay on the hard floor. She tried to imagine the feeling of Patrick's arms wrapped around her, his warm, muscled body pressed close to hers. She closed her eyes tightly, willing him to come back to her.

Darkness crept in at the window. She heard an owl in the forest and the breeze gently moving the trees, and the frightened thump of her own heart.

She woke at the sound of an engine revving and sat up instantly. It was a small, tinny sound. She scrambled out of the sleeping bag and looked out of the high window. The little red car was disappearing down the avenue of trees, the tail-lights winking at her in the misty dawn.

She flew down the stairs barefooted, flung back the front doors and ran down the cold stone steps, out onto the path through the woods to Patrick's cottage.

She burst through his front door and then recoiled as a strange perfume assaulted her senses. She sniffed. A peculiar scent had invaded the cottage. She stood and listened for any sound. She had half expected him to be standing there waiting for her but the living room was deserted. She shivered in the cool atmosphere and walked over to the stove to warm her hands. It was cold. The fire wasn't alight and it was obvious that it hadn't been alight all night. There were two empty mugs in the sink. One of them had a dark smear of red lipstick along the rim. She shuddered and carried on, straight through to his bedroom.

The covers were pulled tight over the bed. There was no indent on either pillow. His mobile phone lay on the bedside cupboard. Then with a great sigh of relief, she realized that she was once again surrounded by Patrick's musky, woodsy scent. Perhaps he had walked to the Chateau to wave off his wife and by some strange chance she had missed him. She turned around and was about to walk out of his bedroom, their bedroom, when she noticed an envelope on the dresser. It had her name on the front.

Scarcely breathing, she picked it up and opened it. There was a short note inside.

Ellen,

I am so sorry. I have to go. I know I should wait and explain everything to you, but I didn't want to wake you and I didn't want Diane to cause a scene. Things have become impossible for me to put off any longer. I don't know when I will be back, but I promise that I will contact you as soon as I have any news. I don't want to go, but there are some things that are unavoidable and some things I need to change. I have decided to go back to England with

Diane and get everything sorted out permanently. Please forgive me for leaving you like this.

Patrick.

She looked aghast at the letter and then read it over again. She didn't know what it meant. *Did he mean he was leaving her permanently? What things were impossible?* She didn't understand any of it.

The tears started to run down her face as she stood there. They gathered on her cheeks and then dripped from her chin onto the floor. She scrunched the letter up in her hand and then shoved it in her pocket. She looked around their bedroom through tear filled eyes. It was the room that she had spent the best weeks of her whole life in, the only room that she ever wanted to sleep in. She turned back towards the door. If Patrick wasn't here then there was nothing here for her.

She walked slowly across the living room and was about to leave when she noticed his old coat hanging on the back of the door. She lifted it to her face and pulled in a huge breath. His scent surrounded her, filled her. She pulled the coat over her cold, shivering shoulders and then carefully shut the front door behind her. She couldn't lock the door, there had never been a key, she just closed it firmly as though shutting a section of her life away in a closed room and began the long, slow walk back to the Chateau.

She didn't rush. What was there to rush for? There was nothing here for her without him. The whole forest felt empty, desolate. Not even the birds sang.

It was only as she neared the Chateau that she heard her name being called and a great chatter of voices, mingled with huge bellows of laughter.

She had completely forgotten about David. He had arrived with five of his friends to test out their hotel. They were expecting her to make every effort to impress and then they were going to rip the Chateau apart with their criticisms so that the whole place would be perfect before she opened her doors to the paying public.

She quickened her pace, not ready to see them, but as the situation was unavoidable, she braced her shoulders and ran the rest of the path.

David was at the base of the steps, calling her name, while a pressure-masked Joe unloaded bags from their two jeeps. Adam was negotiating his wheelchair up the newly concreted ramp and Paul tapped his way up the steps with his white stick. James hobbled about on his crutches as Gemma struggled with the bags Joe shoved at her feet.

Gemma threw a bag towards the steps.

"Hey! Just because I'm the only girl doesn't

mean you can make me do all the fetching and carrying." She was protesting loudly. "Why don't we tip Adam out of his chair and put all the bags in that? We can come back for Adam later. If we feel like it." She added. There was a howl of laughter from the men and Adam spun the wheels of his chair away up the ramp as Gemma lunged after him, grabbing the back of his seat with a metal hand.

Adam strained in her grasp but eventually gave up and let his chair roll backwards.

"Oi Cheeky! You only caught me 'cos I swear that new arm of yours is longer than your real one. I'm going to complain, gives you an unfair advantage. Hey Dave! Where is she? I haven't seen Ellen in ages and I'm dying for a kiss." Adam was looking towards the Chateau.

"I'm here!" Ellen called out of the nearest trees. "Sorry I wasn't here to meet you. I had someone…Something I needed to sort out." Her voice faltered as they all turned towards her.

David came towards her immediately, a lopsided smile on his scarred face.

"Hey! There you are. How are you?" He stopped half way across the driveway. The smile dropped. "Ellen! You've been crying!" His voice was suddenly full of concern as he noticed her swollen cheeks and puffy eyes. "What's going on? What's the matter? Why aren't you wearing any shoes?" They were suddenly all surrounding her.

She looked at all their worried faces. Scarred faces, ruined faces, ruined bodies, ruined lives. She was the only whole one amongst them, but she felt as though all of her insides had been ripped out. And then the whole world began to spin. The ground came up to meet her as David flailed with his arms, shouted her name and failed to catch her as the whole world went black before her eyes.

She woke up, half lying, half sitting on one of the huge settees in the lounge. Gemma was beside her, her real arm gently around Ellen's shoulder, the men were gathered in front of them. David immediately began firing questions.

"Ellen, what's happened? Are you ill? Has that bloody idiot Justin been hassling you again?"

She struggled to sit upright.

"No, please don't worry about me. I was just being silly. I'd had a bit of a …well, a disappointment…Nothing to do with Justin. I haven't seen him since the time he threatened me, and he should be getting his money about now anyway. He has no reason to bother me anymore." She tried to take a deep breath, but the air just wouldn't fill her lungs and then she was suddenly sobbing uncontrollably.

Six huge white handkerchiefs were

immediately waving under her nose. She laughed wetly as she took two, and more tears leaked out of her eyes.

"You lot are going to think I'm such a fool. I can't believe I'm behaving like this…Oh you might as well know, I've fallen in love with someone. I thought he loved me too, but it seems it was just a fling for him. He's gone back to his wife. She arrived yesterday to take him home. He left me a note." She pulled the crumpled letter from her pocket and handed it to Gemma.

Gemma read it quietly, her eyes narrowing as she reached the end, and then passed it on. David read the note aloud to them all. He pulled a strange face as the men all looked at one another.

Gemma sat up straight and looked expectantly around at them, waiting for one of them to explain. There was a stunned silence before she spoke again.

"Well? What does that load of crap mean?" She had never been one to mince her words. "Come on you lot. Tell us ladies here. Is that rubbish man talk for "I'm ditching you"? Is he coming back or what?" She looked around at the men. They all shrugged together and she squeezed Ellen gently. "Do you even know where he's gone?" Gemma looked very confused.

Ellen shook her head.

"I don't know. He said he hadn't seen his wife for years. He was in the army, but he resigned after he was blown up. She left him when she saw what the bomb had done to him. I don't know why she did. It's not that bad. Nothing worse than you lot have suffered. He helped me when I was hopelessly lost the first time I was here and I instantly fell in love with him. I know he came from Essex, but I have no idea where. We were so happy here, the subject never came up and I never felt the need to ask. It's not as though I'm going back and I thought he was going to stay here permanently too." She began the whole story.

Twenty minutes later they were all still staring at her, their expressions grim.

"The bastard!" David snarled. "You mean you've been together since you got all the planning permissions, and now he's gone without saying a word to you. With his wife!" David's incredulous voice shot up a pitch or two in frustration. "God! Ellen, whatever were you thinking of. You shouldn't have become involved with a married man. He was just taking advantage of you. You know the phrase…Having his cake and eating it. He's just a pile of crap."

Paul scrabbled for Ellen's hand, missing it completely and then squeezing it gently when Gemma guided him to it at last.

"What regiment was the shit in? Some one will know him, I'm damn sure about that. He won't get away with this Ellen. He needs to be taught a lesson in manners."

An arm pulled Paul backwards.

"If he comes back and messes you around again, I'll smash what's left of his face." Joe was speaking through his mask, his teeth clenched.

There was a sudden commotion as Adam forced his way forwards.

"Christ! He hasn't got his hands on your money, has he?" He rolled his chair between Joe and David, pushing them aside.

Ellen waved them all down.

"No, please. He's not like that at all. I never even told him about the money. Another subject never seemed to crop up. He's not a bit like Justin. He assumed I've convinced the bank to stump up the money for the renovations and I never bothered to correct him."

She dried her eyes yet again. Their indignation on her behalf was more touching than she could bear. They all stood around her, limbs missing or useless, faces distorted, all ready to defend her honour at a moment's notice. They were all muttering angrily.

She tried to calm them.

"No! Please. It's entirely my fault. I made

the first move. Patrick had told me he was married and I ignored that. I assumed that because she had left him, he wasn't interested in her any more. We've only been serious for three months. Well, I was serious. I thought he was serious too. Don't blame him please. And he'll have to come back at some time. He owns the house in the grounds. He can't just dessert it." She looked up at their worried faces began to get up. She couldn't let her ruined romance spoil their precious week off. "What a terrible welcome for you all. I'm so sorry. It wasn't meant to be like this. It's not going to be like this." Her voice was becoming stronger. "You lot have one week to tell me what I need to do to this place, so go on... don't hang around here. Go and find somewhere to sleep. Adam, the lift's over there and your room's first on the left. It's the only one fitted with a specialist bed and I need to know what you think of it. I have someone coming in to help you later if you need it. The rest of you will have to make do with put you ups I'm afraid...Paul stop! You're heading the wrong way, show him will you Gemma. I'm going to start preparing breakfast. Get yourselves sorted and back down here in half an hour. Last one back down does the washing up!" Adam blasted his chair towards the lift and the others all bolted for the stairs.

Chapter Eight

Breakfast was brunch before it was eaten. They threatened to roll Adam down the stairs when he moaned that he'd only had to wash up because the lift was so slow. His first suggestion was that she buy a dishwasher as soon as possible. Their laughter rang through the Chateau as they moved from room to room, discussing advantages and ideas.

The vast gardens were another adventure. The forest echoed with their shouts as they scared the wildlife and then all got soaked in the river as they cleared the banks ready for fishing huts. They even pulled a protesting Adam from his chair and sent him floating off on a couple of tied logs, to find the best area for a canoe school. They all had plans for outdoor activities. Ellen began a list. Every day something new was added.

The week passed quickly and they presented Ellen with a huge variety of suggestions at the end of it. They sat and had dinner "en famille" around the huge dining room table the night before they all left. The wine flowed and the banter was endless. Ellen wondered how she was going to cope with the quiet once they had gone.

"I don't know what I'm going to do without you lot." Her voice trembled slightly as she cleared the long table for the last time.

David gathered vegetable dishes and followed her through to the kitchen. He helped her load the newly purchased industrial sized dishwasher. He looked up quickly as he heard her sniff.

"Hey Sis! Come on. Cheer up. I'll be back before you know it." He pulled her into a huge bear hug.

Ellen snuggled into his shoulder.

"I'm going to miss you all so much. It's been such a fun week. I'm going to be so bored." She wailed into his pullover.

David laughed aloud.

"Are you mad! You still have a load to do. Especially if you start on the stables and riding school. The self-catering apartments are a good idea too, but only if we can manage them properly. What do you think of the time schedule for opening? Still on for Christmas?" He wiped his finger under her eye.

Ellen shrugged.

"Maybe. But I thought that perhaps New Year might be better. Any guests won't have to worry about bringing presents for the kids. And then only if I can get the staff trained up in time. I'm going to be sending every one of them on paramedic or first aid courses before we open. I'm beginning the first interviews in two weeks, though I think I'm going to ask Geraldine to stay on anyway. She already has a nursing degree and she's been fabulous with Adam. We've had a lot of applications for the other positions. I'm starting with eight full time staff and I have three part time jobs lined up. I hope to increase that when we know what sort of numbers to expect. We haven't had anyone apply for the chef's job yet. I was surprised, the French are always telling us British how awful our food is, but it turns out that no one really cooks here. You just go down to the market, buy it already done for you, heat it up, et Voila! Dinner!" She laughed. "If I can't find anyone suitable, I'll go to the market myself and dish it all up the same as the locals do. It'll work out expensive but I can manage like that for a while." She smiled at his look of horror.

"Do you want your guests to come back? I thought we were trying to give them a taste of the high life." He gave her a friendly shove on the shoulder.

"Cheek! You haven't complained all week, just shovelled it all in and scraped the plates clean." She laughed at him.

He shrugged.

"Well that's what us army guys do. Gotta eat when you can get it. Whatever it is. Never know how long you might have to go without."

"It'll be a doddle then. I have the local

farmer lined up to supply pigs for the hog roast and he's going to help set up the farm too." She was feeling slightly better. "I wish your next leave was sooner. You could come and help with the farm." The idea had been Joe's and everyone had agreed that it was a super suggestion.

David leaned back on the kitchen table.

"Maybe I will." He was mysterious.

Ellen shook her head at her brother.

"How? You only have leave every six months. We'll be up and running by then." She pulled a chair out and sat down looking glum again.

David grinned at her.

"I was keeping it as a surprise, but you may as well know now. I'm getting out. Adam and James are too. We've had enough and the army are offering us a good redundancy package, not that I need the money of course, but the others do. Adam wants to spend more time with his wife and kids. His body is getting worse. The paralysis really sods you up. He doesn't think he's going to reach old age, and James has to have another set of operations on his legs. He almost wishes they had chopped them off in the first place, they give him so much trouble. If they don't get any better this time, he says he's going for amputation. I don't envy him. At least I had no choice. I've told him to think about it long and hard first."

Ellen grabbed hold of her brother's hands and squeezed them gently. Tears leaked out of her eyes.

"Oh David, I can't believe it. When do you finish?"

"Nine weeks. And that's not the only thing, Joe's finishing his five years in three months. He's not signing up for any more. He's thinking of asking you for a job here. He doesn't think he'll get much anywhere else, what with his face the way it is. I said I didn't think he would have any problems at all, the bomb blast has made an improvement." He laughed aloud at Ellen's shocked expression. "If he does ask you, for God's sake don't offer him the chef's position. His cooking is worse than yours."

Ellen smiled indulgently, knowing his banter was serious for all his jests.

"This is the best news ever. What about Gemma and Paul. Are they getting out too?"

"Paul's staying in, he's got two years left to go. He's absolutely brilliant at all the coded stuff. He says it's even easier to read them now that he can't see the words, makes him think, use his brain more. They have offered him some new robotic eye system, but he has to be in still to get on the scheme. It's all experimental, but he's fine with it. Like he says, it's not as if you can get more blind than blind. And he gets paid to do it too." He gave Ellen another squeeze.

"Gemma loves the job as you know. As soon as she gets the all clear she's getting back into the field. She's already passed the physical and just has to get through the endurance testing. I don't think there's any chance that she's going to fail." He stood back up straight. "Only just over two months and I'll be free. I never expected to want to come out. I loved it while I was in the thick of things and thought I was going to be in the army for life, but stuff like this," He looked down at his legs. "It gives one a new perspective on everything."

They began walking towards the kitchen door together. Ellen smiled up at him.

"Come straight back here when you've finished, and tell Joe to come too, as soon as he's out. We'll get him doing all the outside activities. He'll absolutely love it." She was holding David's arm as they walked across the hall and she squeezed it gently. "Thank you David. I feel so much more positive now."

"Good. Let me know how you're getting on with the interviews. I'll ring when I can and I'll see if I can organize some guests for New Year. We won't have time to get much advertising done this side of Christmas." He kissed her on the top of her head as they reached the stairs and he pulled the end of her plait playfully. His hand caught on her clip.

"Still wearing it then?"

She smiled up at him

"Of course. I love it and wear it nearly every day. I still have the original one too. It looks a bit grotty in comparison to this one, but I'd never get rid of it"

He dropped her hair.

"Perhaps I should buy you a different one, you must be fed up of this design."

"Never, but I won't say no to a pair of matching earrings. There, that's made my birthday easy for you. Now get on up to bed, you've got a lot of travelling tomorrow."

"We're leaving really early in the morning, so don't get up especially. I'll see you in a couple of months."

She gave him a huge cuddle.

"Can't wait. Don't forget to tell Joe he has a job waiting too. Take care and I'll see you in a few weeks."

Chapter Nine

"Holy Shit!" David whooped. "This is fantastic! When did you think of it? I don't remember anyone suggesting anything like it." He was hanging onto the zip wire about to launch himself into midair. His breath was puffing out in huge clouds as he worked himself up for his descent.

Ellen looked worriedly down into the ravine.

"I thought of it myself after I'd climbed down those dreadful steps to the fishing huts for about the fifth time. They're really steep and they kill the backs of your legs. There's no way you could do it very often, and if you go down via the track, it takes ages. You don't have to use that thing David, I put it in for the kids really, you can go down in the cable car, the same as most adults would." She looked at his grinning face.

"Not on your life. This is going to be great. What's it going to be like at the bottom?" He was peering downwards, slightly dubious for a second.

"Messy if you don't hit the break in time." She nodded at a small red button on one of the handles. "It has an auto brake but it's geared for someone a lot lighter than you. Your weight will take you too far and you'll hit the water. And you are meant to be wearing that safety harness you idiot."

David grinned gleefully.

"Don't be ridiculous! You know what we've been through! The danger is the whole point surely! And the brakes, well you can forget them. This'll be a walk in the park!" And with a great *"Woo Hoo!"* He was gone.

Ellen walked to the cable car, the lines of which ran adjacent to the zip wire, and pressed the descend button. She made a more sedate pace to the beach at the bottom of the ravine. She could hear loud laughter echoing around the the valley.

"That was brilliant." David puffed up to her and opened the door of the cable car. His trousers were soaked and great clouds of breath were coming out of his mouth. "I haven't done anything like that for years."

"You're just a big kid." She smiled, glad that he was enjoying himself. "The tree top walk goes in next week. And the canoes and rafts for the white water rafting arrive the week after. Joe is going to have his work cut out for him when he arrives. I hope he's up to it." They began to walk along the river. Ellen pointed out the fishing cabins, tucked a little back from the bank.

David had arrived the evening before and had been amazed at the amount of work that had been done in such a short space of time. The rooms had all been decorated and fitted out in sumptuous style. No one would guess that the four posters all had hidden hoists or pressure relief mattresses. The ensuite bathrooms had wet room showers and sunken hydro-therapy baths, every one of them big enough and with ramps or lifting gear to take a wheelchair and still leave room for an assistant.

All the furnishings were of the most beautiful quality, the materials rich and enticing. The library was stocked with innumerable shelves of books. The games room was complete with table tennis, snooker and card tables. The cinema took up part of the attic space while the cellar swimming pool had fabulous underwater mood lighting, along with landscaped ramps and hoists. All the treatment rooms were filled with delicious smelling lotions and rubs. Ellen had made one of the cellar rooms into a gym, equipped with all the latest high tech machinery plus several racks of old fashioned weights, and another into a beauty parlour with a hairdresser, beautician and nail expert, while beside the pool, she had installed an integral sauna room with an icy cold shower. She had fitted a squash court and two badminton courts in the old riding school and five self-catering suites in the stables.

"You've done brilliantly Ellen. The whole place is wonderful! Has everyone confirmed for New Year?"

"Well it's mostly your mates, but I've had a

couple of families who had just heard about it. They want to be all together so I'm putting them in the self-catering suites. They can all have separate bedrooms there, but still be with each other and they're all going to be eating with us up here. I'm hoping to get recommendations from them all. And then there's the Maire, his wife, plus all my workers and half the town coming too for the celebration dinner. There are going to be over a hundred of us in the ballroom on New Year's Eve, sort of grand opening gesture I think."

He bent and picked up a flat stone, weighed it in his hand before he skimmed it across the water.

"Great. I can't believe how well you have done already. And how's the budget going? Are we overspent by much?" Ellen had discussed the figures with him the evening before, over dinner, but David had been more preoccupied, flirting furiously with Geraldine, one of her specialized staff who was helping out all round. He had been so entranced as she had waited at the table he hadn't really listened to Ellen at all.

"Not too much. Twenty eight thousand at the last count. It sounds like a massive amount but it's only because of the additional accommodation. I'm getting a few bookings for later on in the year and we have the first of three weekends of corporate guests arriving at the end of January. They are fully booked and paying the full going rate for all of the rooms so I've nearly made up the difference already. If they recommend us to other business clients, I'm hoping all the corporate weeks will be filled completely. They are only happening one week in six but will pay for the entire shortfall with our other guests. I'm relying on Joe to organize all the team building activities before then. I must make a note to remind him that the corporate stuff will be for normal human beings and not for a load of adrenaline junkies like you lot. I don't want them put off because he's making them try and leap over a twelve foot wall." She sounded a little flat.

David looked over at her, wondering whether he should bring the conversation up.

"Joe'll find that a doddle, it's right up his street…" He stared into her sad eyes. "Not still fretting over that scumbag that let you down, I hope?" He put a reassuring hand on her shoulder.

She smiled weakly and lied badly.

"No, don't be silly. I haven't had a moment to think about him. I have a hotel to open in less than a month and there are still a million things to do."

David stared down at his sister as she turned to face him.

"You are such a bad liar Ellen…You are skinny and listless and have obviously been working all the hours God sent, just to keep your mind off him. I knew you were still upset when we left before, but I had no idea that you were in so deep."

She turned away from his scrutiny, her voice was almost strangled when she replied.

"Deeper than you'll ever know David. I'll never get involved with another man again. No one could come close." She stared into the distance and blinked hard as she thought of Patrick.

David picked up another stone and hefted it in his hand.

"I just can't see how he'd drop everything like this. I mean, it's been months now. His house must be a right mess.

Ellen didn't dare look back up at David. She couldn't tell him that before he had arrived she had spent every night at Patrick's house, sleeping in his bed and snuggling up to his coat, desperate for anything of him, any tiny infinitesimal shred of him, to hold onto.

She nearly cried out at the thoughts. She quickly changed the subject.

"Come on, I'm going back up to the house. I need to speak to Geraldine about the other bar staff she's booked and I also need to sort out the first aid exams. I have three staff taking them this week. And you need to get out of those wet clothes. You must be freezing." David's trousers were flapping wetly against his legs.

He looked down at the dripping fabric, completely unconcerned.

"Huh! Don't see why you would think that. I haven't got any legs to freeze." He grinned as she rolled her eyes and they turned to make their way back to the cable car. "Not nearly so exciting as going down." He muttered darkly as they rose slowly through the trees.

They spent the next three weeks ironing out minor problems and training all the staff in emergency first aid, regardless of their official position.

Joe arrived on Christmas Eve, tired and thin and more than relieved to be out of the services.

He slugged back another glass of delicious fine wine and sat back in his chair obviously very relaxed.

"It was hell there last week. I've been to that many goodbye parties. I've barely eaten a thing, only drunk barrels of cheap beer. I feel like it's all still sloshing about inside me. I shall need feeding up before I start work here." His speech was slightly slurred.

David laughed out loud.

"Well you've come to the wrong place then. Ellen's doing all the cooking as we still can't find a real chef. She's interviewed a couple, but they're all into that nouvelle cuisine here. Useless for us lot. This is a hotel for chaps with massive appetites. Ellen's going to stick with the roasts and buffets for a bit. She can just about manage them." He winked at his sister.

"Cheek! You haven't complained much, just scoffed the lot and you should see what we're having for tomorrow's dinner. It's going to be fabulous. Geraldine's been no end of help and I'm loads better at it all." Ellen looked indignant.

Joe looked up, suddenly very interested.

"Ah! Would that be the lovely Geraldine that I've heard so much about? I swear she was here before looking after Adam, but I barely took any notice then. I wondered why Adam kept coming down to breakfast with a massive grin." He smiled at Ellen's puzzled expression. "David has been giving me daily updates on her, via email. I've heard all about her fabulous green eyes and glossy dark hair." He ducked as David threw a roast potato at him. It landed further down the table leaving a trail of grease across the tablecloth. "Have you still got her helping you with your legs every morning and night?" Joe leaned across, stabbed the potato with his fork and popped it in his mouth.

Ellen gaped at David.

"What? Helping you with your legs? You haven't David!" She stared, aghast at her brother.

David blustered, looking as though he were about to kill Joe.

"No, no. I was just kidding Joe about that, though I may have mentioned her eyes once or twice." David protested his innocence and then concentrated very hard on his roast beef and Yorkshire puddings.

They finished dinner with a delicious almond cake from the market, smothered in crème fraiche. Geraldine came in, green eyed and dark haired, with a tray of coffee. Ellen smiled as she saw her wink at David before gliding away again into the kitchen.

Joe let out a great guffaw of laughter, but then stopped quickly as he registered David's glare.

"By the way." He changed the subject swiftly. "I saw that terrible ex-fiancé of yours last week. That awful blond guy. Justin was it? He said you had invited him over for a stay. He said something about a reconciliation. I didn't think you would get back together with him. I was a bit surprised."

Ellen's jaw dropped and she nearly choked on her mouthful of coffee before she spoke.

"Surprised! So am I. I've not seen him for months and I've certainly not invited him over. The last time I had any contact with him was about the sale of my Spanish apartments. I had to write him an enormous cheque just to get him off my back. You must have been mistaken Joe. I don't want anything to do with him ever again."

Joe smiled grimly.

"I knew he was talking out of his backside. Ghastly bloke, bit creepy. I was glad when you split up. Can't think why you ever went out with him in the first place. I was a little drunk at the party. I must have misheard him. Oh well." He yawned widely. "I think I'm going to get an early night. It's been a long day what with all the travel. I can't wait to have a look over the grounds and see what you have planned for me." Joe pushed his chair back and stood up.

"I'm going to go to bed too Ellen." David finished his coffee and levered himself out of the chair. He winced as he rose. "God! I think I've jarred my back going down that zip wire." He rubbed the base of his spine.

Ellen rolled her eyes in despair.

"Serves you right. You've been down it about thirty times this week alone. It's meant for the kids, you great idiot." She looked exasperated at him.

David let out a laugh.

"I was testing it out, making sure it's safe." His eyes twinkled merrily at her.

Joe was nodding eagerly at David.

"Yes, Dave has been telling me all about it and I agree. You can't test out that kind of thing enough. I think I'll have to test it too. You know, just to make sure." They were both grinning widely.

Ellen shook her head in defeat.

"Oh, do what you like. You're like a bunch of kids, but don't come moaning to me when you're in agony from being so reckless." She picked up the remaining dishes and took them through to the kitchen.

She heard David and Joe making their way up the stairs. She filled the dishwasher and turned it on, then turned off all the lights and followed them up the stairs.

She walked along the corridor towards her own room, but stopped as she heard David groan as she passed his door.

Perhaps he really had hurt his back? She sighed deeply, opened the door and stepped in to check on him.

She stopped instantly as she saw Geraldine sitting on the edge of the bed beside David. She looked as though she was tucking him in. He was half under the covers, his scarred chest showing just above the quilt. The two of them stared silently at her. Then Geraldine slid her hands out from under the sheets and pulled out one of David's false legs.

Ellen glowered at David, who stared back at

her, guilt written all over his face.

"For God's sake David! You weren't joking." Ellen hissed at him. "Taking off your legs is not in Geraldine's contract. She has enough to do without pandering to you." She looked over at Geraldine and smiled apologetically. "Don't believe him when he says he can't manage. He's a rotten liar. And David, you can get up in the morning and make breakfast for everyone for taking advantage. And you can bring me a tea up here too. I don't take any sugar." She slammed out of the room and stalked to the room at the end of the corridor.

She turned the door handle and crept inside. There was a small camp bed pushed against the wall between some boxes. Her sleeping bag was laid on the top and over that was Patrick's coat. She was about to get undressed when there was a gentle knock at the door.

David walked in, both legs back in situ, his pyjama jacket on but unbuttoned and the trousers slightly askew where he had obviously dragged them on in a hurry.

Ellen slumped.

"What now David? I'm tired. I'm sorry I was sharp, but really, taking your legs off indeed! Whatever are you going to get the poor girl to do next?" She folded her cardigan over the back of a small chair.

David walked to the chair and sat down.

"You really should knock before you barge in Ellen…" He paused briefly. "She wasn't taking my legs off." He looked at the floor and then glanced back up at Ellen, hoping he wouldn't have to elucidate further.

She raised her eyebrows.

"Really! So what was she doing then, straightening your sheets and tucking you in? You'll be getting her to make you hot chocolate and read you bedtime stories next."

David coughed into his palm.

"Don't be silly, it's just that she…she was, well I was…" He paused again and stared hard at his sister. Ellen just looked right back at him, waiting. He rolled his eyes and took a deep breath. "Well, if you want me to spell it out for you. She wasn't straightening the sheets Ellen, she was helping me straighten something else entirely." His tone was significant and he squared his shoulders as he glared at her. He twiddled his thumbs and sat with his hands in his lap while he watched her expression as she suddenly caught on.

Her mouth fell open and she felt herself flush to the roots of her hair.

"Oh God! I am so Sorry! I thought it was all just a load of flirting. I had no idea you were actually involved. Why didn't you tell me sooner? How embarrassing." She covered her face with her hands.

David laughed, relieved that he hadn't needed to be even more explicit.

"Embarrassing! Bad luck for me more like. I was about to have the best Christmas Eve of my life. She's gone back to her own room now. She was mortified." He smiled gently at Ellen who was also looking mortified. "Look, we were going to tell you, but it's only been three weeks and I just hadn't got round to it. I liked her before when we came but she was only helping Adam and he had all her attention then, but this time, well I didn't want to say anything if we weren't sure about each other. We've been emailing and speaking on the phone all autumn. I adore her Ellen and I don't know how, but somehow she seems to adore me too. Even with only half a body and less than half of a face. It's just as well that I've still got all the most interesting bits of me left. And I don't mean just my brain!" He grinned sheepishly.

Ellen laughed and wrapped her arms around his shoulders.

"Oh David! I'm so glad for you." Her eyes were shining.

He let out a relieved breath.

"Yes, well, I'm going to put a lock on that door tomorrow morning and knock from now on eh." He glanced around Ellen's room suddenly taking in the lack of furnishings and a proper bed. "Why are you sleeping in here anyway? This is just a box room. Why haven't you sorted out your own bedroom yet?" And then he noticed the big coat. "Oh Ellen, you had been sleeping at his place, hadn't you? Good God, I've been here for nearly a month and I was so wrapped up in Geraldine I didn't notice that you were practically sleeping rough. Had you been down at his place until I arrived?"

She gulped and nodded, tears suddenly springing into her eyes, desolation in her heart.

"I couldn't help myself. I wanted to be with him so much, I did the only thing I could think of to be near him. I wanted to be there if he came back."

David pulled a handkerchief from his pyjama pocket and handed it to her.

"But what if he comes back with his wife? You have to give this up Ellen. He hasn't made any sort of contact. He's not interested. He would have written or something if he was."

Ellen gulped loudly and stifled the tears.

"I know. I know, I just didn't think it would be so hard without him. If he had just told me it was over, I would have felt better about it. It's the not knowing. His letter was so vague." She wiped her eyes on the back of her hand and blew her nose in David's handkerchief.

"I think he's made it pretty clear by now,

don't you?" David was firm.

"Yes, I know. I'm just being pathetic." She sighed. "Don't worry. I'll get this room fixed up properly. I won't go back to his place again." She closed her eyes and took a deep breath.

David grunted in approval.

"Good. Have you any of your stuff there?" She nodded silently, her heart hurting so much that words wouldn't come. He grabbed her hand and squeezed it tightly "I'll go and get it all for you over the next few days. I don't want you going back there and being all upset again. We have too much to organize here. I tell you what, I'll go down there when you go to buy the pig for the New Year's hog roast. Then you won't even think about it. You'll be too busy working out how to cook the blooming great thing." He stood up, ready to leave.

She chanced a few words, praying she could hold in the tears.

"Thanks David. And I'm sorry about earlier again. I didn't mean to ruin your evening."

David laughed again.

"Don't worry, I'm pretty sure there will be plenty of other opportunities for her to practice her techniques. Oh, and you can bring me my tea in the morning, just to make it up, two sugars please." And he left the room chuckling lightly.

Chapter Ten

Patrick turned the light on and dumped his bag on the settee. *God! Nearly New Year's Eve.* He sighed in relief, glad to be home. The last few months had been a complete nightmare.

He shivered. The house was colder than he had hoped. He wasn't expecting Ellen to be right there waiting for him, but he had hoped that she had left a fire going. He rested his hand over the stove. It was stone cold. He opened the door and peered in at the ash. It was clogged and damp. He stood up straight and looked around at the rest of the house. He frowned, slightly confused. There was a thin layer of dust over all of the surfaces.

It wasn't that there was dust that disturbed him. He didn't care about a bit of dirt. In some ways he rather liked it. It made everywhere seem more homely and normal, but this was all wrong. There was no way Ellen would have allowed their home to become cold and dusty. He walked into the bedroom. It was cold too. He sat down on the bed and pressed his hand to the quilt. It was slightly damp.

His heart started to thump hard and for a moment he was worried, but then he sighed in relief as he thought he knew what must have happened. She was probably busy up at the Chateau. Perhaps she had opened the hotel for Christmas and was now coping with left over guests. She probably had more arriving for New Year too.

He stood up again and walked back to light the stove. She would be tired when she eventually arrived home. He would get a fire going, make it warm and cosy for when she got back.

The flames grew a little higher and he watched as the smoke churned up the chimney. The fire was warming the house quickly. He walked back to his bedroom and pulled the quilt back to let the sheets air. A wonderful waft of her perfume floated up to him. He pressed his face to the pillow, breathing in the fragrance he loved so much. He sat for a while waiting to hear the door open, but as the heat permeated the room he stood up and pulled off his clothes. He took off his leg, then lay down on the bed and wrapped himself in her scent. God, he was so tired from the journey. He wished he'd hired a car. The ferry and then the trains and then the taxi, had taken forever. He breathed in deeply again and closed his eyes. He couldn't wait for her to come and find him. He was desperate to have her back in his bed. `

He curled up in the slightly damp covers, anticipation and desire warming him more than the flames of the fire in the room next door.

Ellen woke early. She shivered in the early

morning light. The central heating hadn't kicked in and she felt very cold as she pulled on her dressing gown. She made a mental note to keep it turned on during the night when she had guests. She wandered to the bathroom thinking about her conversation with David a few nights before. He was right. She had to move on. He was picking up her bits from Patrick's cottage that morning. Ellen had wanted to go herself, but David had insisted that she wasn't to go back. She had given him a list of the things she had left there.

She stood in the shower lathering her hair and watching the suds gather in the drain before swirling away. It was New Year's Eve. The last day of the old year. She wouldn't be sorry to see it go.

She dried quickly and then walked back to her bedroom and pulled on her jeans and jumper. The room had changed in the few days since David had discovered her sleeping rough between a load of unpacked boxes. He and Joe had spent Christmas day lugging the boxes up to the attic and moving furniture. Then they had spent Boxing Day painting the room before a new bed had arrived.

Ellen brushed her hair and fastened it, then dabbed on a little lipstick. She didn't have to dress up early, she had to go and collect the pig anyway. She'd put her glad rags on later just before the party started. She walked out of the door and down to the kitchen.

Geraldine was already there with two mugs of tea in her hands. She had moved into David's room on Christmas day. She smiled a little self-consciously at Ellen.

Ellen smiled back.

"So he's got you fetching him tea now too. He's such a lazy devil. Don't let him get away with it Geraldine. Get him to make the tea for you. He's perfectly capable." She pulled a mug down from the shelf for herself.

Geraldine sipped out of one of the mugs.

"I think I will buy a kettle for our room. 'e loves a cup of tea first thing I the morning, I think it is an English custom, but now I like it too. I think I will let him be lazy a little longer. I don't mind. I love him." She said it so simply that a tear sprang to Ellen's eyes.

"Yes, he said. You are both so lucky to have found one another. I know he thought it would never happen, not after being so injured. Some people can't see deeper than the surface."

Geraldine's smile grew wider.

"David is a very intense person. I saw that straight away, and I find him 'andsome too. A few scars don't bother me, not when the person inside is so wonderful. 'e tells me you felt the same about that man that lived 'ere."

Ellen gulped, surprised at Geraldine's openness.

"Yes, I did, but unfortunately for me, he's gone. I don't think he's coming back and even if he does, it won't be the same as you and David. Patrick has a wife already. I'm putting it all behind me as of today. You know, a New Year and a new beginning, besides what with all our guests arriving today, I doubt I'll have time to be maudlin over it."

Geraldine nodded.

"Yes, and of course there will be all these 'andsome soldiers arriving. Who knows, there may be someone else in your life very soon." She swept out of the kitchen doors.

Ellen looked down, suddenly more miserable than ever.

"No," She whispered. "No, there won't be. Not ever again." She turned and filled her mug with hot water.

Patrick turned over in his bed. For a moment he was disorientated and it took him a couple of seconds to realize where he was. A weak sunshine was shining through his window. He hadn't closed the curtains the night before. He swivelled himself round, pulled on his leg and stood up. He peered out of the window and the pushed it open wide. Crisp, clean air flooded over him. He looked out over his overgrown vegetable garden and into the nearest trees. He breathed in deeply. He could smell the lush forest around him, the scent of pine and earth. He smiled. It was good to be home.

He pulled some clean clothes out of his bag and dragged them on. He was going to have to go to the Chateau pretty soon. She still wasn't here and the suspense was killing him.

He turned to his room and noticed the thin layer of dust on the dressing table again. He walked over to it and ran his finger along the surface, then stopped as his finger touched a bottle of Ellen's perfume. He smiled and was about to walk through to the kitchen to make tea when he heard his front door open.

Relief swept over him. He hadn't realized how anxious he had been feeling, but she was here at last! He threw himself back into the bed, grinning stupidly as he pulled the covers over himself, waiting for her to come and discover him. And then he couldn't help himself.

"Hey! Ellen, I'm in here, come and get me!" He yelled delightedly.

There was complete silence from the room next door for a few seconds, and then the unfamiliar sound of heavy, charging feet on the floorboards. The bedroom door flew open. Patrick flung out his arms in welcome and waited expectantly for Ellen to leap on him.

He didn't expect a six-foot blaze of fury to launch itself across the room at him.

He leapt out of the bed again, stumbling against the chest of drawers.

"Who the hell are you? Get out of my house!" It took a second for him to realize that the man facing him, with steam practically coming out of his ears, was scarred a lot worse than himself. He was truly terrible to look at. His nose was ruined and misshapen, one dark brown eye was half closed, but the other was glaring at him furiously. The way the man lurched as he came across the room made it obvious that he was a double amputee. Realization suddenly came to him.

"David?" Patrick pulled himself away from the furniture and questioned urgently. "Are you David? Where's Ellen? Is she at the Chateau?" He tried to smile but it wavered as David came further into the room.

"You've got a nerve, you piece of shit! Why the hell have you come back?" David spat the words, his breath coming in furious gasps. "She's just getting over you. You stay away from her, do you hear?" His words hissed from the side of his scarred mouth.

Patrick staggered on his feet, completely confused.

"What! Getting over me? What do you mean? Why isn't she here?" He was so taken aback that he sat down on the bed again.

David started yelling.

"Why, you bastard! Don't pretend you don't know. She not here because you left her! After months of using her, you just waltz off with your wife, leaving her completely devastated. One pathetic note that's left her hanging on for months, desperate for you to come back. You're lucky I don't kill you right now."

Patrick shot up. David was coming closer, fists clenched now, but Patrick leapt forward from the bed and faced him.

"One note? What the hell are you talking about? I've written every bloody week telling her what's happening. I was living in one shitty B and B after another wondering why she hadn't written back. I had assumed she was busy." He scratched his head.

David was still puffing.

"Don't lie to me. She's worked herself half to death to get this place up and running in time for tonight, just to get over you, and you walk in here like nothing has happened. Did your wife chuck you out again? Is that why you've come back? Well don't think you can just start where you left off with Ellen. It's not going to happen. She doesn't want anything to do with you. You go near her ever again and I will kill you. Do you understand? And don't think I can't, because I bloody well can. You stay away from her. Okay?"

Patrick was a good few inches taller than David, but David's fury was greater. Patrick shook his head, trying to keep calm. Fear gripped him. The muscles in his chest had constricted so tightly he wondered how he was still breathing. His voice was almost strangled in his throat.

"I'll stay away if she tells me to, but not you. You can go to hell and back before I do anything you want. Is she at the Chateau? I'll go up there now and see what she says. If she doesn't want me, then fair enough, I'll go, but not until I've heard it from her lips." He pushed past David and strode out of the door.

Patrick could hear David lumbering after him, but he didn't turn around. He had to see Ellen immediately. He had to get this sorted out and explain. He couldn't let her leave him. David wouldn't have to kill him. He'd do it himself if she didn't want him.

David struggled to keep up as Patrick surged ahead along the path. He marched straight up the stone steps of the Chateau and pounded through the front doors.

Geraldine screamed in shock as the doors

blasted inwards, and she dropped a vase of flowers and greenery that she was carrying across the hallway.

"Mon Dieu! What 'as 'appened?" She was breathless with fright.

Joe burst out of the lounge door at her scream, he skidded on the broken vase and puddle of water, only just managing to keep upright. He flailed around, finding his feet just as David puffed in through the doors behind Patrick.

Joe was about to ask what was going on, when he stopped dead and stared, open mouthed, at Patrick. Then in one fluid motion, he pulled himself up to attention and saluted.

David staggered to a stop behind Patrick and gawped at Joe. Joe was still rigid.

"What the hell are you doing Joe? This is the scumbag that let my sister down." David's breathing was laboured. Joe never even blinked. He stayed firmly at attention.

"At ease Lieutenant!" Patrick barked at Joe. "Where's Ellen?"

Joe gave the merest flick of his eyes over at David and then back to Patrick.

"Sir, Not here Sir!" Joe had dropped the salute but was still in full military mode. He made his complete report. "Her fiancé arrived shortly after Captain Phillips went to fetch Miss Ellen's stuff, Sir!

A taxi dropped him off. She was going to go and pick up the pig for the hog roast. Her fiancé went with her, I saw him get into her car, Sir." He was still standing very straight.

David moved forwards, pushing past Patrick's now frozen form. He clutched Joe's shoulders, shaking him out of his rigid stance.

"Joe, do you mean Justin?" David exploded. "What was he doing here? He's just a money grabbing low life. She dumped him way before she bought this place and he certainly wasn't invited here today. He's not her fiancé Joe. She detests him."

Patrick slumped forwards, suddenly breathing again. Joe looked taken aback.

"But he said he was, Dave. You remember, I told you before Christmas, just after I arrived. I saw him at one of my leaving parties. He said he had been invited over, he said they were getting back together."

David rolled his eyes.

"You were drunk at that party you idiot! And you downed a load of wine the evening you arrived here too. Ellen wouldn't get back with that piece of crap if he were the last man on earth. If you had been sober you would have known that he was telling you a load of lies." David was fuming at Joe.

Patrick marched across the hall, poked his

head around the door of the lounge and scanned quickly. Then he was moving along the hall towards the kitchen. He wasn't sure if he believed Joe or not. He felt it was best to check. He pushed the door open and looked around the room. It was empty. The kitchen table was set up to deal with the pig. A long metal prong and the block of knives that were waiting to be used, sat at one end. The middle knife was missing from the block.

It wasn't on the table.

He scanned round the rest of the units, then the sink and finally the huge dishwasher. It wasn't there either. Patrick felt the blood drain from his face, he spun back round and was about to go back to the hall, when his boot kicked something across the floor.

A million sparkles leapt around the room, Patrick bent down to pick the object up, just as David, and Joe entered the room together.

"That's her clip! The replacement of the paste one you gave her years ago Dave!" Joe yelled.

Patrick felt as though he were about to pass out. Never in a million lifetimes would she leave this on the floor. Never in another million lifetimes would she drop it and not notice. All three of them stared at it hopelessly.

The telephone rang and Geraldine answered it. She gabbled away in French for a few moments then she put the phone down. She turned to the men, her expression frightened.

"That was Monsieur Lefevre. Ellen 'asn't been for the pig. 'e wondered if we still wanted it. 'e says Ellen told 'im that she would be there early as 'e 'as to go out. I told 'im that she must have been delayed, but 'e can't wait in any longer. 'e is going to drop it off on his way to the market."

There was a shocked silence. Then Patrick spoke quietly as he looked over at David. His expression showed nothing of how he was feeling. His voice was like solid stone.

"This Justin bloke, is that the blond guy she came here with originally?" David nodded. Patrick held the clip up to the light. It glittered at them. "It's beautiful." He said to no one in particular. He was silent for a heartbeat, thinking hard, then he cleared his throat. "I saw him arguing with her the night we first met and I showed Justin up here a few weeks later. I didn't really take any notice of him at the time, but then he told me that they were engaged. I was so jealous I didn't listen to Ellen when she tried to explain about him…Actually I wanted to kill him, the thought of him touching her, sleeping with…" His teeth ground together and he didn't finish, but looked at David and Joe darkly. They stared back at him silently. "Well anyway." He carried on. "She said he had threatened her over some money problems." His voice was hollow. "I wish she'd told me how bad it was. I'm not completely broke, I might have been able to help her if she had asked." He lifted his chin at David. "Does she owe him much?"

David gawped at him, unable to believe what he was hearing.

"Ellen doesn't owe anyone a penny. In fact she gave him a small fortune in Spanish property just after they split up. The idiot sold it all without finding out about the tax laws first. He lost the lot and expected Ellen to pay him off again." David glanced over at Joe and then back to Patrick. "She said that she never got round to telling you. Patrick, Ellen is a millionairess. Our Aunt left us both a fortune. Ellen has put nearly everything she owns into this place. Oh God! That must be it. Justin's property mad, he's kidnapped her to get the Chateau." David looked as though he was about to collapse.

Patrick was looking at Joe again.

"Half an hour ago they left here in her car? Anything else you remember?" Patrick was horribly calm.

Joe thought for a moment racking his brains, knowing that every detail was significant.

"Justin said he was helping her with the pig. They walked out arm in arm. Ellen didn't say a thing, so I assumed she was okay with it. I bet he had that missing knife aimed at her. God! I wish I'd thought it through. He's a complete jerk. There's no way she would have asked him to help her. He wouldn't know a pig from a pineapple." His tone was bitter.

Patrick was thinking hard.

"I didn't hear any car on the road past the cottage, and I'd been awake for a short while before you arrived. Did you see or hear anything before you got to my cottage David?"

David shook his head emphatically.

"No, they must have gone down the avenue or they would have come past me as I went to fetch her things."

Geraldine interrupted quickly.

"They didn't go past me. I was cutting ivy for the table decorations down by the gates. I only arrived back 'ere ten minutes ago to put the finishing touches to my display and 'er car was gone by then. They must 'ave gone via the river crossing, that's the only other route out, but that won't work either. It's in full flood this time of year. They can't cross it in Ellen's tiny car. They must be 'ere somewhere on the estate still."

Patrick started for the door. His face was set, his manner strangely calm. His self-control was frightening.

"I'm going after them. David, can I take your car?" His tone was neutral, but David recognized the order in the question.

David marched after Patrick, all hatred of the man forgotten as he worried about his sister. If Patrick was going to help get her back then that was fine with him. He'd deal with the rest later.

"No, I've got a better idea. Joe, you take the car and cut off the track back from the river. Do whatever it takes, but don't let them come back past you. If he gets off the estate with her, we'll never find him. Patrick, you come with me. I know a quicker way down to the river. It takes us right to the crossing." David threw his keys to Joe, grabbed Patrick's arm and pulled him through the doorway.

They heard Joe speeding off in the car as they jogged along the path to the ravine. David was finding the going hard but Patrick pulled him along.

David was looking at the tall, powerful man, striding along just in front of him.

"You've had something done to your leg? Ellen said you limped with the one you had before." He was breathing heavily.

Patrick didn't slow down at all. He pounded on up the path.

"Got the new model. It's fantastic, at least as good as the real thing, well you can see. It was one of the things I was sorting out while I was away;

it was a bastard to get used to after over two years in the old one. It works in a completely new way and you have to compensate with your body. I had to have loads of physio on my back, but it's worth it in the end. I told Ellen all about it in my letters." Patrick had reached a fork in the path and waited for David to point out the direction.

David panted up, drawing in deep breaths.

"Ellen hasn't had any letters from you. I told you that." They started down the next path and it soon widened into a long plateau. Patrick stopped dead and gasped as he saw the top of the zip wire. He ran over to it.

"Well, I've been posting them every week. They can't all have been lost. Damn, when did you get this thing put in? It looks fantastic." His voice was lost in admiration for the zip wire. He reached up and pulled on the bars, testing the tension.

David tried to look displeased, but his anger was no longer focused on the man in front of him.

"Ages ago. Ellen said the stone steps down to the river were just too steep and she thought the kids would like this more. Kids be blowed, it's fantastic fun, but more to the point, it's also very fast. Takes less than ten seconds to get to the bottom if you don't bother with the brake. Don't tell Ellen, but I've been tweaking it a bit. You know…The tension and all that. We'll have to loosen it off a bit when the guests arrive. I wouldn't want anyone to get hurt. It's strung out as tight as it can be right now. Makes it phenomenally quick. Bit of a thwack at the bottom is its only disadvantage. Kills your back, and you're definitely going to get wet." David peered over the edge of the ravine. "Look, down there." His voice was quiet now.

Patrick looked down and forgot absolutely everything else as he saw Ellen standing at the edge of the surging river. Her face was the colour of chalk, her huge dark eyes obvious in her pale skin. Her long hair was floating about her in the breeze. If she hadn't looked so petrified, she would have looked simply perfect. A deep groan of longing rose up in his throat.

And then a man stepped in front of her, obscuring his view. For a second Patrick wanted to shout to the man to get out of the way and then he suddenly remembered why they were all here. He could see that the man's hair was blonde. Justin was holding Ellen's arm tightly. He was staring at the river. He raised his free arm as though about to strike Ellen with the back of his hand. Patrick let out a growl of pure fury and grabbed hold of the metal bar above his head.

Justin was glaring into the surging, swirling water. It was making waves as it raced down the river. It was obviously way too deep for Ellen's car. They would have been lucky to get across in David's Land Rover. He wanted to slap her. He held her in tight to his side, the kitchen knife pressed against her ribs, somehow resisting the urge to stab it deeply into her flesh.

"You little bitch! You knew we wouldn't be able to get across. Well, don't think this is going to help you at all. I was going to ask you for more cash, but seeing you all alone like that and with those knives all so handy, well, you can't blame me for taking a chance. I was thinking of holding you to ransom, but why bother now. I can just slice you up a bit and shove you in here. It's rough enough, nobody will ever be able to tell if you've been stabbed or not. I can forge your signature easily. I'll just write out a will in my favour. It will be believed, after all, you gave me all that other property. Everyone will think that it was your dying wish that I inherited everything." Justin was speaking in low menacing tones.

Ellen was shaking with fear, staring up at him, watching his contorted face. She couldn't believe this was happening to her. He had appeared in the kitchen from nowhere and she had felt more than uncomfortable as soon as he had mentioned more money, but she hadn't expected him to grab a kitchen knife and kidnap her. He looked positively deranged.

She tried to buy some time. If it didn't take David too long to pack her things, then he would be up here straight away to play on the zip wire. He couldn't resist the thing. He'd see them from the launch point instantly.

"Please Justin. Can't we talk about this? Perhaps we can come to some arrangement. I can give you more money, I don't need to make out a new will." She knew she sounded desperate.

"Well you won't be the one making it, will you?" He pushed her forwards a little more and she twisted away from the river. She didn't stand a chance in the rampaging water. She turned right around, feeling the knife slice against her jumper.

The heel of her boot dangled over nothing. She staggered forwards and tried to move to the side, but Justin moved with her, stepping back as he held the heavy knife out in front of him now, its evil point jutting into her stomach.

"You just don't get it do you Ellen. I've had enough of being poor. I want your money and I don't just want a bit. I want it all, David's too if I can get it, and I want this Chateau. It's wasted on you and your mangled friends. I won't be satisfied until I have everything." He was sneering at her.

Ellen was determined not to cry. She lifted her chin defiantly, trying with everything she had, not to succumb to tears.

"I don't understand why you're doing this. I gave you so much. It wasn't my fault that you threw it away, but I'm willing to overlook that and help you again. You can have the money, but you're not getting the Chateau." She looked up at him and noticed the coldness in his eyes.

And then she noticed something else. A huge dark shape was moving swiftly through the air, just above and to the left of Justin's hairline. She glanced down at the ground again, praying that he hadn't seen her surprised expression, praying that he wouldn't turn around for another few seconds. She took another step to the left, hoping he would follow, just as she saw the wire above their heads begin to tremble. Then she stepped smartly back to the right as a whizzing sound could suddenly be heard.

Justin looked confused at her for a second more, and then he spun round towards the sound, just in time to catch Patrick's huge feet right in the middle of his chest as he hurtled down the zip wire.

All the breath was punched out of Justin's lungs and he was catapulted into the air. Patrick's momentum carried them on, tumbling them both into the boiling water. Patrick instantly planted his feet on the bottom of the river, standing firm in the swirling waves. He didn't lose a second. He grabbed the back of Justin's jacket, before he could be swept away, then he shoved his head deep under the water. He held him there, breathing hard, his blue eyes like glaciers of ice, his expression frightening, until Justin stopped thrashing about.

Ellen suddenly came to her senses and shouted.

"Patrick don't. Please don't drown him. He's not worth it. Let him up." Her voice was strained, trembling.

Patrick stared up at her. He caught his breath as he saw her tiny figure, trembling on the riverbank. She was shivering with fright, nearly fainting with the surprise of seeing him. And then all the anger left him. She was right. He would spend the rest of his life in prison if the man died. He'd only just escaped from one sort of prison, one of his own making, he couldn't be shut up in another. He lugged Justin up again and flopped him to the bank. The man's head bobbed around for a second and then he started spluttering as he tried to sit up.

There was more of the whizzing sound and then David hit the water with a huge splash. He moved towards the riverbank and launched himself at Justin, landing a massive punch to the man's nose. Justin was still woozy from the smack in the chest and the dunking in cold water. The punch on the nose finished him. He slipped off the riverbank and back below the surface of the river.

Patrick pulled him up again and threw him back onto dry land, where he lay, his nose bleeding, gasping like a stranded fish.

Joe roared up in David's car. He slammed on the brakes, leapt out and pulled Ellen back from the water's edge. Then he leaned over and stuck his hand out to David, hauled him up the muddy bank then went back for Patrick. He saluted again and then stuck out his hand to help. Patrick waved him away as he climbed out of the surging, chest high torrent.

Ellen had fallen against David's soaking body. She was shaking so violently her teeth were rattling.

David pulled her into his arms, holding her tight to him.

"Come on, let's get you back home. Patrick, can you and Joe deal with this pile of scum? Bring him back to the Chateau. I've somewhere we can keep him until we decide what to do with him."

Patrick looked at Ellen for a long, silent moment and then nodded once. He bent and picked Justin up by the back of his soaking collar and dragged him towards David's car.

Chapter Eleven

Geraldine was bringing steaming mugs of tea to the kitchen table. Joe and David were sitting either side of Ellen. They were waiting for Patrick. He had volunteered to take Justin to the cellar and lock him in one of the rooms. Patrick was a little unhappy to discover that the rooms were now comfortable and clean. He would have much preferred to chain the man to the wall, or string him up by his thumbs.

Joe nodded his thanks to Geraldine and heaped in three spoonful's of sugar. He stirred the tea vigorously.

"Thank God Reeves was here. We might not have even seen the clip if he hadn't kicked it. And he handled that zip wire like a pro. I bet he hasn't done that in a few years." Joe slurped his tea and pushed a mug towards Ellen. She was still shaking, looking dazed and confused. The mug shook in her hand, tea slopped onto the table and she put the mug down again. Geraldine wiped a cloth across the spilled tea.

David wrapped his hands around his cup and leaned forwards to give Geraldine a kiss of thanks.

"Yeah, maybe, he was pretty good on it, but what the hell is all that saluting stuff about Joe? I know he's been in the army but it's all a bit over the top now." David was watching the door carefully.

Joe wiped his mouth and spoke in an exaggerated whisper.

"I can't help it. It's automatic. He outranks me and you too for that matter. Major Pat Reeves. You probably don't know him, not being in the same regiment, but I do. He was one of my commanding officers for a time, before he was put in to lead a Special Forces team. Bravest man I ever saw. We used to call him Super, as in "Superman". It started out because of his name, you know, Reeves, like the film star, but it soon meant something else. He seemed completely invincible. You should have seen him in Afghanistan. He really was like the "Man of Steel" He was awarded the Victoria Cross two years ago for his outstanding bravery, but only received it in December. He didn't think he had deserved it because he thought it was his fault that his patrol was blown up in the first place. Rubbish of course." Joe was watching the door too. "He managed to save the rest of his men even after having his leg blown to smithereens. They were about to take out a group of warlords, when a roadside bomb went off. Same sort of thing that did for me." Joe brushed his face with his hand. "The shrapnel massacred his leg and covered the lot of them in this vile burning fluid the bastards were using then. The whole patrol were injured horribly, and the hostiles were down on them in seconds, but somehow he managed to strap his leg and fight them all off single-handed. Shot seven of them and killed the last two with his bare hands apparently. Then, even when he must have been in agony himself, he administered as much first aid to his chaps as was possible. He kept the men together and himself functioning until they could raise some help. My mate Alex was there, said his whole stomach was literally hanging out. Reeves shoved it all back in and sat there for over three hours holding the wound together. Alex knows that he would never have survived without Reeves. About a month ago he was eventually persuaded to accept the medal, had to go to Buckingham Palace for it."

David gulped and glanced nervously towards the door.

"Christ! The man's a hero! And I called him a shit and threatened to kill him. I might have to apologize. Depends on what he's got to say about himself and what he's been doing for the last few months." He frowned a little.

Joe raised his eyebrows in surprise.

"I doubt if you could kill him. He's much more likely to kill you. He's had a load of special training. His group were the elite. Hard as nails, all of them, and him more than the rest. As to what he's been doing, he's been getting himself divorced. It was all round the office. There was a right old "hoo har" because he didn't want his awful wife at the medal ceremony. He said they were divorced, but she denied it. Apparently she was making all kinds of fuss about it. She reckoned she was entitled, but he wasn't having any of it, said he'd rather not have the medal if she was going to be there. Wouldn't accept it until the divorce was finalized and she agreed not to go. Apparently the Queen was not amused with his ex-wife's antics and she agreed to the delay."

David pinched the top of his nose and grimaced.

"God! Now I feel really terrible. If only we'd known all this earlier. How come you didn't tell us about him before?" David looked accusingly at Joe.

Joe shrugged expansively.

"Well I didn't know it was him before, did I? I don't have a crystal ball. Nobody gave me a photo or anything. He'd dropped off the radar completely after the bomb. We all just thought he'd been pensioned off. Or perhaps his injuries were too bad for him to come back. None of us could contact him, we didn't know he'd moved out here and when we saw Ellen earlier on in the year, he'd already gone back. We didn't see him at all. I don't remember his last name being mentioned either,

Ellen only referred to a Patrick. But that wouldn't have helped much either. I don't think anyone ever called him that in the regiment, we only ever used his nick name so it just didn't click." Joe defended himself miserably.

The door opened and Patrick strode into the kitchen.

David and Joe immediately leapt out of their chairs, stood to attention and saluted.

Patrick gawped at them and waved them down quickly. They fidgeted uncomfortably before sitting again. Patrick walked towards the table.

"Would you stop doing that. We're not in the army now. I don't want you to salute me every time I appear. It's embarrassing." He pulled out the chair opposite Ellen and sat down himself. He grabbed a mug of tea and wrapped his hands around it. He was still wearing his wet clothes and he shivered as the heat of the mug warmed his hands. "Ellen, tell us what happened earlier. We need to know." His tone was gentle and warm.

Ellen looked up from the table slowly. She had been listening to David and Joe trying to comprehend that they were talking about the man now sitting in front of her. She stared at him, still not quite believing he was there. Then she glanced over at David, feeling very nervous. He picked up her hand and squeezed it reassuringly.

She looked back to Patrick.

"David had gone to get my things from your cottage. Justin came through to the kitchen only five minutes after he'd gone. I didn't hear him arrive or anything. He was just suddenly there by the door. I was setting up the table so I was ready for the pig." She shook a little and then carried on. "I don't know what his plan was when he first arrived, but he took one look at what I was doing and had the knife in my side in a second. I though he was going to cut me." She sobbed with renewed fright. David scowled murderously. Ellen choked before she carried on. "I had to go with him. The only thing I could think of doing, to leave a clue that I was in trouble, was to tug out my hair clip. I knew David would know that something was wrong immediately. I left it on the table, but it caught the light. Justin saw it and was furious. He hates it." She looked up at David. "He doesn't even know that it's real. He thinks it's the original one you gave me years ago, David. He threw it onto the floor and dragged me away. I didn't know where it had landed and I didn't think you would find it. When Joe just waved us off, I was terrified. I knew if we left the estate you would have no idea where he had taken me." She stopped and shuddered violently.

David put his hands around her arms and rubbed them up and down.

"Patrick nearly stood on the clip. We all knew something was wrong immediately, it wasn't just me that noticed. It was as good as any distress flare. But why did you direct him to the river? You were trapped down there. It doesn't seem very logical."

She looked at her brother patiently.

"I thought it would be the first place you would go after you had finished clearing my things. You've been mucking about on that zip wire every day for weeks, trying to get it to go faster. It's practically on free fall now, you've pulled the wire so tight. If you had got back here and found I was out and not asking you to do anything in particular, even if you hadn't seen the clip, you'd be up there like a shot for a bit of fun."

David laughed out loud at being found out so easily.

"Ha! Got me, but actually it might have been more difficult if Patrick hadn't been at home when I went down there. He was expecting you to leap into bed with him so was a bit shocked to see me. He came charging straight up here to find you. We reasoned it out between us because nobody had seen the car go past. I hadn't heard a thing while I was going to the cottage and Patrick had been awake for a while before that. He hadn't heard anything either. Geraldine had the avenue covered picking flowery stuff, so that just left the track to the river crossing. I had Joe block the road and Patrick and I went to take the quickest way down."

Patrick laughed at David.

"Quick! That's the understatement of the year. It's so fast I nearly crapped myself. Last time I did anything like that was back in my first lot of training." He smiled at the memory but was suddenly quiet again. He reached out a long finger tentatively, and touched the back Ellen's hand. "Ellen, David says that you don't want me anymore, that you haven't had my letters. I can't believe it, I've sent so many. He says you'd given up on me. Please tell me it's not true." His voice was suddenly strained to the point of breaking. "Ellen, for God's sake tell me."

Ellen wiped a tear that had sprung to the corner of her eye.

"I didn't know what to think any longer. I didn't know what your original letter meant. You had just gone off with your wife and I thought that you weren't coming back. I haven't had any letters from you Patrick. I thought that you must have got back together with her."

He wiped his hand across the side of his face. He glanced between Joe and David, his expression strained.

"I just don't understand it. I'm not lying about this. After I realized that I had left my phone behind I decided that it wasn't worth buying a new one. I didn't think I was going to be quite this long and I swear I wrote every week. I even asked Ellen to come for the medal thing with me, but then I heard some my old mates talking about your hotel. One of them was thinking of booking. I just assumed you must be so busy that you didn't have time to reply or because I've stayed in a few different places, I may have missed your replies. What with the new leg and all, I even went back to my parents for a week, so I was thinking that perhaps your letters hadn't caught up with me. It never crossed my mind that you thought I wasn't coming back for you."

Joe scratched his head.

"We all read your first letter mate. It was pretty crap. I didn't have a clue what you were going on about, sounded like a load of old boll..." He stopped and shrank back as Patrick nearly leapt out of his chair. David jumped up and pushed Patrick's chest hard with the flat of his hand. He glowered for him to calm down and then nodded back at Joe, who carried on nervously. "But whatever you wrote then, I still I don't get it. If it was Afghanistan, I could understand a few letters being mislaid, but here? This is France, and while I know it's a little old fashioned, it's not as if we're in the back end of a war torn, God forsaken country. Are you sure you've got the right address?"

Patrick raised his eyebrows at him.

"Of course I've got the right bloody address. I've lost my leg not my brains. I know where I live." He sounded more than a little exasperated.

Geraldine suddenly gasped and flapped her hands excitedly. They all looked up at her. She started gabbling on in rapid French.

"Mais, l'address n' est pas la meme d' ici. Chez toi, ce n'est pas Le Chateau." David stopped her as Joe looked very confused. She carried on in English. "Your address. Why 'ave you been writing to your address, when Ellen lives 'ere? They are not the same place you know." There was silence around the table.

Ellen shook her head.

"But I've looked in the box every day. I've had loads of other letters. Including some of Patrick's own mail. There's been nothing from Patrick."

Geraldine sighed.

"But that is because the cottage never used to 'ave a separate address. Now, since you 'ave made this 'otel and given Monsieur Patrick 'is own land, the cottage 'as its own box. It is on the track out by the road. I 'ave seen it myself when I go to the market. You 'ave checked that one?" It was obvious that Ellen hadn't. "La! I will go and look now." Geraldine turned and ran out of the door.

Ellen looked around the table miserably.

"Well, why would I look anywhere else? I didn't even know you had your own box." She looked at Patrick accusingly. "I assumed everything of yours came here. And why would you send letters there anyway?" Tears were now running down her face. Joe passed her his handkerchief.

Patrick took her hand from David and massaged her palm with his thumb.

"I put up my own box after you signed all the land over to me. I put it in one day when you were out looking at furniture. And I sent the letters to our house, because it was our home. We'd been there together for weeks Ellen. You didn't even have a bed up here, so why would I send them anywhere else?" He spoke so gently, so sincerely that Joe turned away and studied the floor with determined concentration.

Ellen was still doubtful.

"But you left with your wife. I thought you had gone back to her. She was so beautiful, so elegant, and the way she kissed you! What else was I meant to think? Why did she come and ruin everything anyway?" Her tone was accusing.

Patrick pushed the chair back and sat up straight, his sudden anger visible.

"Yes, she is beautiful, but only on the outside. On the inside she's as ugly as hell. She only came over because I'd received a letter at our old home about my compensation. She'd opened it and found out how much I was going to get. It's a lot. Not that it will ever make up for this." He brushed his hand down the ruined side of his face. "She saw it as a good excuse for a spending spree. But the money came directly to me. I'd not told anyone except my parents that I was here and she contacted with me still. They gave my address up straight away because they want me to be happy again. And she also found out that I'd received the commendation for a medal. I hadn't told her before. I didn't even want the damn thing. My men were ripped apart because of the mistake I made." He hung his head. "I'd done the recon on the position, but it was a trap, the sneaky little shits sneaked in after us and placed the bomb. I wouldn't have had to clear up the mess if I'd been more careful. Not that that seems to have made any difference. For some reason my men all loved me still and forwarded the commendation. Someone must have told Diane about it. She couldn't see herself on the arm of a cripple, but a hero, well that was another thing entirely. I hadn't seen her since the day she left me in that awful hospital. She couldn't even look at me then. Her rejection of me was worse than the actual injury. You can never get over a thing like that. I was so hurt and angry, I never wanted to see her again. I still never want to see her again."

David grunted.

"I've heard of that sort of thing happening before. Some women just can't take it."

Patrick looked over at him, aghast at his words.

"You have? Well I hadn't. It's enough to kill a guy. I pity anyone else that's ever had to go through it. All of my mates, my team, were still with their wives no matter what had happened to them. Stuck with them through thick and thin. It's not easy being an Army wife. Lots of pressure, but Diane and I had been together a long while, nearly ten years. I thought she would be okay with it. I'll never forget the look on her face when she saw me at the hospital. I mean, I knew it was going to be hard for her. I expected a few tears. I didn't expect revulsion." He hung his head. "She couldn't even look at me properly. She didn't come back again. I just had a letter to say that all my gear was being moved to my parent's house. She didn't want to be with a disabled man. But of course, money makes a big difference to some people. I couldn't believe I hadn't noticed it before. She was all over me as soon as she thought she might get a few quid. She makes me sick to my stomach." He finished bitterly.

Ellen was aghast.

"How could she do that to you? How could anyone?"

Joe looked up again. Ellen could see his eyes were watering. She handed him back his handkerchief.

Joe gulped and his voice trembled.

"Patrick has always been a hero Ellen, even before this big medal he was a legend in the ranks. It was as if he was completely invincible. It's a lot to live up to and maybe Patrick's wife liked the heroics. Maybe she thought that having disabilities would change him. Perhaps she couldn't see past them to the man inside. Not everyone is like you Ellen. You have an inner strength that sees past the surface, Geraldine too." He nodded at David. "Some of my mates have had a hell of an ordeal with their partners. That's why I love the idea of this hotel. I hate it when people stare at me as if I'm just some kind of freak. I thought I was lucky not having a wife or girlfriend to reject me. Must be awful." He blew what was left of his nose his nose loudly.

Patrick nodded at Joe, suddenly desperately grateful to the man in front of him. He looked over to David.

"I came out here nearly three years ago just wanting to hide, to be left alone. I didn't want to see another soul ever again, but then I met Ellen, God!

I'll never forget the effect she had on me. I nearly went mad with desire, but I thought she would be revolted by me. I couldn't take rejection like that ever again, so I avoided her for months." Patrick's eyes were full of pain, his voice thick with emotion, "I couldn't believe it when she told me how she really felt. I nearly blew it and sent her away, but we got it right in the end. Ellen saved me from the life of complete misery I was wrapping myself in. I was so in love with her, the three months together were the best of my whole life. And then Diane turned up and ruined everything. Even though I hadn't seen her after the hospital, I'd filed for divorce, but there's a two-year wait if there's no adultery involved. When she came here in September, she said she had changed her mind, that she still loved me and she wasn't going to agree to a divorce now. I could have told her about being with Ellen but I didn't want to drag her name into it and fortunately for me I only had to wait another month and we'd been officially apart for over two years. There was no way she could stop it even if she wasn't happy with my plans. I only had to wait a few days and then apply for the 'decree absolute' but even that takes six weeks from application." He finished bitterly.

The door suddenly opened again and Geraldine came through with a pile of damp, mouldering mail.

"There!" She said triumphantly. "You 'ave written so many. And I can smell your perfume on them too. You are such a romantic man." She smiled widely at Patrick. "Some 'ave been there a very long time and 'ave been eaten by the snails, perhaps they like the perfume too Monsieur, but the rest are still fine. Patrick 'as told you the truth Ellen. 'e 'as sent you many letters of love." She dumped the pile in front of Ellen.

Ellen looked up at Patrick. His eyes were burning into hers. She swallowed before she could speak.

"I feel so stupid, faithless even. I am so sorry for not believing in you. I don't know what to say." She looked down at the pile of letters and moved her hand to pick one up.

Patrick quickly put his hand over hers and held it still. She looked back up at him curiously.

"Don't look at them now. Please. I was a bit sentimental in some of them. Save them until later. I wouldn't want these two," he tipped his head towards David and Joe, "thinking that I'd gone soft."

David let out a great guffaw.

"Soft! Bloody hell! You were like a machine when you thought Ellen was in danger. I was almost scared of you myself. That reminds me, what are we going to do with that scumbag in the cellar. Shall we just leave him there to rot?"

Patrick snarled.

"I did think of that at first, but I think your guests may object to the smell. I came up with a better plan. I've already told him what's going to happen if he ever bothers us or any other woman again. I told him that we'd seek him out, wherever he tries to hide himself, and then we will cut off selected parts of his anatomy with a blunt chainsaw. Slowly." He grinned as he saw David wince. "I'm pretty sure I convinced him that I was perfectly serious, but I think we should let him sweat on it for a couple of days before we let him go. Or we could just attach him to the hog roast. The rest of your guests may find that a bit of fun. We could let them baste him and then tell them that his squealing is the cabaret."

Ellen giggled, then stopped and slapped her hand to her forehead.

"Oh hell! The pig! I haven't been to pick it up. I don't even know what to do with the thing once I get it here. The hotel guests will be arriving at five for the grand opening tour, and the celebration dinner is at seven…it's never going to be done in time." She wailed hopelessly.

Patrick looked at her and took immediate control.

"Right. Now don't panic everyone. I think the porker is being delivered fairly soon, from what

Geraldine said of the phone call earlier. Do you know how much it weighs? I can work out the cooking time now and if you have some sage, thyme, maybe some honey, mustard and balsamic vinegar anywhere, I can get a marinade ready for the basting. If you have any old bread, I can sort out some leeks and onions from my garden for the stuffing. I'm assuming you have accompaniments to go with it. Potatoes and veg?" Ellen nodded and Patrick carried on. "Good, we can get a huge dauphinoise in the oven. I can make fresh bread later. Joe, can you get the fire going so it's good and hot, lots of red embers and not too much flame? We want there to be plenty of nice crackling. I'll find some bay leaf too, there's a load of bushes round the Chateau. We can burn it on the embers for extra flavour. Oh, and waft some of the smoke in the direction of the cellar, will you? I'll go and tell Justin our alternative plan for him in a minute." He stood up quickly, shoved his sleeves over his elbows and scrubbed his hands in the sink. He whipped a towel from the range and dried his hands, then started for the cupboards.

The others all stared at him open mouthed as he pulled down a selection of ingredients. He was humming absentmindedly as he threw some herbs together in a bowl and then added the honey, mustard and vinegar. He stirred vigorously. It took him a few seconds to notice the quiet behind him.

He turned back to them as their silence grew louder.

"What?" He questioned their unified gaze.

David looked at Ellen, grinned broadly and winked.

"I think we've just found our new chef."

They all jumped as the doorbell rang at that very second and then Monsieur Lefevre was heaving the prepared pig onto the table. Joe went to start the fire and David and Geraldine rushed to find some money and a bottle of brandy for Monsieur Lefevre.

Patrick and Ellen were left alone in the kitchen. They were silent for a few seconds, the only sounds being Patrick mixing things in the bowl. He stopped stirring and turned to brush the pig with the marinade. Ellen watched him silently. When he had finished he put the bowl down and turned to the sink. He washed his hands and dried them again, then he pressed his knuckles onto the work surface. Ellen could see that they were trembling slightly. She came up beside him and lifted her hand to the scarred side of his face. He didn't flinch, just closed his eyes and breathed in deeply, reveling in her touch.

He turned his face slightly and kissed the palm of her hand.

"I thought you would be at home waiting for me." His voice was a whisper. "This place was still a building site when I left. I just assumed you would be living there and knew to look for the mail in my box."

She slid her hand down his neck onto his shoulder and pushed him round to face her. Her eyes were like fire as they burned up at him.

She stepped even closer to him. He could feel her breath on his face as she spoke. Cool and sweet, exactly as he remembered.

"I know that now, and I was there until David came here permanently. I brought your old coat with me when he arrived and I had to stay here. I've slept with it every night since. I couldn't bear to be without you." She put her hand up to his face again.

Patrick thrilled at her touch. His heart began to pound and the pulse in his throat throbbed wildly.

"My divorce came through a couple of weeks ago, but I couldn't chance it getting lost in the Christmas mail. I had to pick up the papers myself. I didn't want them to be delayed over the break. I would have been back before otherwise. My poor mum and dad have had the worst Christmas ever with me there. I just didn't want to be with them and I'm afraid it showed. I'm going to have to invite them over soon. I need to eat a very large portion of humble pie. The ferries only started running again yesterday so I got on the first one back but I had only slept a few hours when David came barging in on me. He said he'd kill me if I went anywhere near you again. He wouldn't have had to Ellen. I nearly died when he said you didn't want me." He was staring deeply into her eyes, wanting her so badly, but afraid to say anything more.

She moved her hand higher until it touched his hair and then she pushed her fingers into the thick dark mass. She sighed deeply.

"He was wrong Patrick. I do want you. I wanted you from the first moment I met you. I love you and I'll always want you."

And then Patrick was at last unfrozen. He lifted his hand and touched her chin with his fingertips. He tilted her face to his.

"Oh God." He sighed, his whole body shaking in anticipation. He bent his head and as lightly as he could, he touched his lips to hers.

She gasped at the sensations that ran through her body as she scrunched her fingers into his hair. Then suddenly his lips were crushing hers with a ferocity she didn't know could exist. His tongue explored her mouth, tasting her greedily. His hands encircled her waist, then travelled slowly over her back. He held her hard to his body. She could feel his heart hammering as though it would burst through his ribs.

When they broke apart, they were

breathless. He kissed her again, more lightly, and then turned reluctantly to the pig, lying on the table.

"It's not that big a beast. It's only going to take about four hours to do on that spit. That leaves us with about two hours spare. I'm still soaked. I'm going to have to go and get changed anyway. It might as well be now. You're damp too you know." He ran his finger down the front of her jumper, letting it rest significantly between her breasts. His eyes were smouldering at her.

She felt her skin burning with desire.

"Do you want any help getting changed? Geraldine helps David take off his legs. She likes spoiling him. Would you like me to spoil you?" She pressed herself as close to him as possible.

A growl sounded deep in Patrick's chest.

"Well, that would be nice, but since I've had this new leg fitted, I don't need to take it off so often. Certainly not for things that are done in the heat of the moment. Well, so they tell me, I've not had the chance to actually test out the theory yet." He caught her lip between his teeth.

She was gasping, barely able to speak.

"So do you want any help then?" She managed to whisper, before Patrick's tongue began tasting her mouth again. He pulled back a fraction, then scooped her up in his arms and shouldered his way out of the kitchen. He carried silently her through the great hall and out of the Chateau straight along the path to his cottage in the woods. He kicked his way through the front door and marched with her into his bedroom. He laid her carefully on the bed and gazed longingly over her whole body.

He answered her at last.

"Do I want any help testing the theory, you mean? Oh God, yes!" And he began tearing off his shirt.

The End

Also Available

by

Jackie Williams

A Perfect Summer

A lifetime of pain and terror wiped out by one perfect summer of love.

Silent Treatment

A young woman's dancing dream while waiting three years for her true love to return from football stardom.

Delicious Desires

A delicious desire for one man could become the love of his life's destruction.

Treasured Dreams

Could a thirteen year old girl's diary have really sealed the fate of her entire family.

Tinted Lenses

She's a photographer's dream, but will those lenses still be tinted by the time they fight their way out of the amazon rain forest.

A Fallen Fortune

Can Leo give up everything he owns for a chance on love?

Forever Scarred (Scarred Series book 2)

Will Joe face up to his fears and let Lucy love him or will his insecurities shove her straight into the arms of her blackmailing boss.

You can see more of all of these books at

www.romanticsuspensebooks.org

Jackie is always available for your questions or comments

Jackiewilliams17@aol.com